'Why are you

Richard saw that [...]
bright, as though she was having difficulty in holding back her tears. That wasn't surprising. For goodness' sake, she'd had a nasty accident. Most women would have wept on his shoulder, but she seemed determined to keep him at a distance.

'Just stay away from me, Richard,' she warned. 'I'm bad news. You don't want to get involved.'

'OK. Do whatever you want.'

Richard walked away. If she didn't want to know, that was fine with him. He was about to get into his car when some instinct made him glance back. Sara was lying on the ground! He raced back to her. Her eyes were closed and she had obviously fainted again.

'You silly little idiot,' Richard muttered, torn between exasperation and concern. 'Just what did you think you were up to?'

He bent down, gathering her up in his arms and carrying her into the brightly lit A&E department.

Anne Herries lives in Cambridge but spends part of the winter in Spain, where she and her husband stay in a pretty resort nestled amid the hills that run from Malaga to Gibraltar. Gazing over a sparkling blue ocean, watching the sunbeams dance like silver confetti on the restless waves, Anne loves to dream up her stories of laughter, tears and romantic lovers. She is already a well-established and loved author with Mills & Boon® Historical Romance™, and *Sara's Secret* is Anne's second novel for Medical Romance™. Writing has been a dream come true—a dream she enjoys sharing with her readers.

Recent Medical Romance™ titles by the same author:

THE MOST PRECIOUS GIFT

And in Historical Romance™:

ROSALYN AND THE SCOUNDREL
A MATTER OF HONOUR
SATAN'S MARK

SARA'S SECRET

BY
ANNE HERRIES

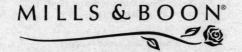

MILLS & BOON®

All the characters in this book have no existence outside the imagination of the author, and have no relation whatsoever to anyone bearing the same name or names. They are not even distantly inspired by any individual known or unknown to the author, and all the incidents are pure invention.

*First published in Great Britain 2001
Harlequin Mills & Boon Limited,
Eton House, 18-24 Paradise Road, Richmond, Surrey TW9 1SR*

© Anne Herries 2001

ISBN 0 263 82660 0

*Set in Times Roman 10½ on 12 pt.
03-0401-51406*

*Printed and bound in Spain
by Litografia Rosés, S.A., Barcelona*

CHAPTER ONE

RICHARD DALTON'S gaze narrowed as he watched the young and very attractive woman at the far side of the room. She was arguing with a man who looked as if he might have drunk too much and was, in Richard's opinion, bordering on the aggressive. Couldn't she see she was making trouble for herself? Or had she been drinking, too? He'd only seen her have one drink, but she could have had others before he'd noticed her.

He was at a party given by a friend of his who lived in Royston, and it was New Year's Eve. People did tend to drink too much at times like these, of course, but something about the woman's behaviour made his spine tingle. She seemed to be searching for something—as if she was unhappy with her situation, was desperately trying to forget something that hurt her. It was a look of appeal in her eyes, a kind of vulnerability about her that struck a chord with him.

He knew all about being hurt, the heartbreak and trouble that could result from a woman being too vulnerable. His eyes were bleak with memories as he watched the woman. Richard thought she was slightly too slender, and her dress ought to carry a health warning, what there was of it. If she kept on this way, she would be in trouble by the end of the evening.

'Why are you frowning? Did someone steal your drink?'

Richard turned to look at the man who had spoken.

They were much the same age, both in their early thirties, and had trained together at the same teaching hospital.

Jonathan Thirstone was in private practice now, successful, confident, and beginning to show the signs of soft living. It was his party. He had invited Richard to his expensive apartment hoping to interest him in working at a private health clinic of which he was part-owner.

'No, I'm fine,' Richard said as Jonathan gestured to the bottle of champagne he was carting around with him. 'Who is that woman, Jon? The one in the silver dress...'

Jonathan glanced across the room, then laughed. 'You wouldn't be interested, Rich. Not your type at all.'

'Interested yourself?'

Richard flicked a strand of hair back out of his eyes. He was thirty-two and his hair was longer than it ought to be, with streaks of grey at the temples. Usually a rich, dark colour, the ends had been bleached to a reddish straw shade by the hot sun of Africa, where he had spent the last year wandering from village to village, administering medical care where he could and making notes for his lecture tour in the States. Now he was back home in England, and considering his future.

'Good grief, no!' Jonathan pulled a face. 'I was just giving you a friendly warning, that's all. Sister Sara Linden has dated a few of the doctors I know, but none of them ever got past first base, if you see what I mean. I'm not sure what's got into her this evening. I've never seen her so argumentative before.'

'I should hope not...' Richard continued to watch as the nurse drank the contents of her glass straight down. The man she had been arguing with grabbed the glass and went off to the bar in search of more drinks. 'She's a fool to herself—she should just walk off and leave him or she'll end up as drunk as he is.'

'Have you thought any more about the offer I made you?' Jonathan asked, uninterested in Sara Linden. 'We need someone like you, Rich. You would fit in very well with our team. Most of the surgical stuff is run-of-the-mill, the kind of thing patients have to wait for on the good old NHS. They are very pleased to get it done in pleasant surroundings, and it's quite lucrative, but your skills with plastic surgery would give us added authority.'

'I'm grateful for the offer,' Richard said, transferring his attention to his friend. 'I will consider the idea, I promise you. At the moment I'm not quite sure what I want to do. I've been offered a grant to do research into AIDS and the likely effect on the future population for a children's charity. As you must know, it continues to be a growing problem in parts of Africa, and they want me because I've had some experience out there. I'm very interested in the project, and I'm not sure whether I want to go back to surgical work. The trouble is, the research project would mean living in America for most of the time, and I had decided I wanted to stay here for the time being.'

'Come to us,' Jonathan said hopefully. 'We're a small clinic but we're up to date and our reputation is growing. Give us a couple of years and then decide whether you want to go back to full-time hospital work.'

'I've been offered several jobs, both private and in the NHS, but I'm still thinking about it. None of them are quite what I'm looking for. Besides, I've promised to do temporary work for a few months,' Richard replied. 'A friend of mine needs a locum for night call-outs. And I have six months before I have to give my answer on the AIDS project.'

'But you were trained as a surgeon,' his friend said, looking puzzled. 'I can understand the research bit—

we're all concerned about AIDS and whether or not there's a time bomb ticking under us—but why waste your skill by temping as a locum for some country practice?'

'That, my friend, is a long story,' Richard said. He was a handsome man, with strong, slightly severe features, his eyes a cool grey that could become wintry on occasion. His mouth set in disapproval as there was a crashing sound as a tray of glasses was overturned. He frowned as he saw that the young woman he had noticed earlier seemed to be caught up in an unpleasant argument with the same man, who was by the look of things even more intoxicated than Richard had first thought. 'Excuse me, I'll get back to you later on the job offer.'

Richard moved swiftly. Unless someone did something, the situation could become ugly. The man was clearly in a temper, and he had a tight grip on the young nurse's arm. She was struggling to free herself, which was how the glasses had been knocked flying, and looked upset.

'Let me go, you brute,' she cried as the man appeared to try and drag her with him. 'I'm not coming with you. I told you, I don't want to see you again. We're finished.'

'You damned...' The man spouted a string of filthy words at her. Her face went white, then red, and then she hit out at him. 'Little cat. I'll teach you...'

Richard got to them just as he was about to hit her. He laid a restraining hand on the other man's shoulder, startling him.

'I wouldn't do that if I were you.'

'What is it to you? I'll hit her if I like. She needs to be taught a lesson.'

'Hit her and I'll break every bone in your body,' Richard said. He spoke in a calm, level tone, but the look in his eyes was enough to make the drunk pause. 'If you're wondering whether I can do it, I should tell you I have a black belt in karate.'

'Go to hell!' the drunk muttered. 'You're welcome to the bitch. She's a lying little…' He spewed out more of his filth, then lurched away.

Richard was looking at the nurse. He saw the way her body was sagging, and knew she was very near to collapse.

'How much have you had?'

'What are you talking about?' she demanded.

'You've been drinking alchohol—don't deny it.'

Her eyes snapped with temper. 'What business is it of yours? This is a party, isn't it? Surely I can have a drink if I want?'

'And the rest,' Richard said, irritated by her manner. If she wasn't drunk why was she responding this way? 'The way you gulped that last one down makes me think it wasn't the first.'

'Go to hell!' Sara turned away, but he caught her arm. She gave him a disdainful look. 'Let go of me, please.'

'I merely asked you a civil question. I thought you might have been drinking and might need help.'

'I've had enough,' she said with a defiant lift of her head. 'Enough to make me forget that men are all selfish devils. But not enough to stop it hurting.' She made as if to go past him. 'I need another drink.'

'I don't think so, Sara. You really shouldn't, you know. It isn't the way. Whatever's upsetting you won't go away because you have a few drinks.'

'What do you know about it?' Sara gave him a bewildered stare, flicking her long, light brown hair back off her face. Who did he think he was—her keeper? She'd had a couple of drinks that evening, but only one of them had been alcoholic. Admittedly, that had gone to her head a little because she hadn't eaten much all day. She'd been too busy on the wards. Besides, it really wasn't his business. Who was he anyway? She was sure she didn't know him. One gin and tonic certainly wasn't enough to make her incapable of recognizing people she knew.

Her eyes narrowed in suspicion. They were a greyish blue with curiously deep irises and very appealing. 'How did you know my name? We haven't met…I don't know who you are.'

'I'm Richard Dalton. Jonathan told me who you were—and I've known what it's like to want to drink yourself into oblivion before now. I've been there, Sara. I know how you're feeling but, believe me, it won't do any good.'

'Well, if you have a drink problem that's your hard luck, but—'

'I don't—but there was a time when I might have if I hadn't fought it.'

Sara blinked and half swayed towards him. She had downed that gin and tonic pretty quickly, but she'd been feeling tired and a bit low in spirits when she'd arrived. It had seemed a good idea to have a few drinks and forget the things that had combined to make her unhappy, but now it had suddenly all turned sour.

'Please, go away and leave me alone,' she said, fighting against the desire to weep on this stranger's remarkably broad shoulders. 'I'm so tired—I just can't think straight. I'm going home.'

'You're not leaving because of him, I hope?' Richard jerked his head in the direction of the drunk. 'You don't want to let that sort ruin your evening.'

A harsh laugh escaped her. 'No! He was just another

of my mistakes. I'm good at picking the wrong sort.' She swallowed hard, blinking back the tears that sparkled in her unusual eyes. 'If you want the plain truth, I'm a mess.'

'You're too hard on yourself.'

'Am I?' She gave him a searching look. 'You have no idea. You don't know me or anything about my life. Didn't you hear what Jeff called me?'

'I don't listen to foul-mouthed drunks,' Richard replied. 'Look, would you like me to take you home?'

'I don't have a home,' Sara said. 'Unless you count the room at the house I share with a couple of friends, that is. A bed, a chair and a wardrobe, and that's about it.'

'No family?'

'Not that you'd notice.' Sara grimaced. Why on earth was she telling him all this? 'You don't want to hear my tale of woe.'

'Try me,' Richard said, giving her a lazy grin. 'If you don't want to go back to your room, why don't we go for a drive and talk? We'll find somewhere to have a coffee and then just drive around until you're feeling better.'

'Why?' Sara's eyes met his in a head-on challenge. If this was just another come-on, she couldn't bear it! Not this evening. Not after what had happened earlier. 'If you want to have sex, I'm not available.'

'I don't want sex,' Richard said, and frowned. 'Not at the moment. Besides, I prefer to do the asking. If I want you, I'll let you know. I was just offering a shoulder to cry on. But if you're not interested…' He moved away. Hardly knowing what she did or why, Sara caught at his sleeve. He turned and seemed to sense the deep unhappiness in her. 'OK. Let's get out of here. Don't worry,

Sara. I shan't suddenly turn nasty and try to compromise you.'

'I know.' She suddenly smiled, a natural smile for the first time since he'd come to her rescue. It was quite a change, as if she'd lit up from inside. 'I've met a few like that, and I can tell in a minute if a man is likely to be dangerous. I feel safe with you.'

'Thanks.' Richard laughed, a deep, husky sound that Sara liked immediately. 'At least, I think that's what I mean—or is it ouch?'

'Oh, you're sexy enough,' Sara murmured as he began to lead her towards the door. 'It's just that I'm off men. I've decided to give up chocolate and dating. It's my New Year's resolution.'

'You're a glutton for punishment,' Richard remarked as they collected their coats from a stand in the hall. 'You'd be better giving up the booze—or at least cutting down.'

Sara was turning up her coat collar. She glanced at him, and her eyes were bleak.

'For goodness' sake! I had one drink, all right? The rest of them were lemonade, because I was thirsty. I've been on the wards from six this morning until six this evening, and we hardly had time for a drink let alone something to eat.' She glared at him. For some reason he had got under her skin. 'Maybe I was planning to have a few more drinks. Surely I have the right to get drunk for once if I want? I have plenty of excuses, believe me!'

'Yes, I can understand that. It happens sometimes— when things hurt too much. I'm sorry if I spoke out of turn. I just didn't want you to get hurt. Life can be lonely sometimes, and it's good to have a friend when you need one.'

Sara looked into Richard's eyes and saw sympathy

there. There was something else, too, and she sensed that he had suffered deeply—and not too long ago.

He was very attractive, she decided, and undoubtedly sexy! She'd noticed him looking at her across the room several times before the unpleasant incident with Jeff, but she'd been feeling too mixed up in her head to respond, even though she'd been aware that he was a very good-looking man. She tried to avoid such men these days. When she dated at all, she tried to choose the ones who looked safe. She'd made a big mistake with Jeff!

'I know it was stupid, but I wanted to forget…' Sara hesitated. What she wanted to forget was too personal, went too deep to tell anyone.

'Yes, I can understand that. It is tempting to drink too much when the pain gets too hard to bear but, believe me, it doesn't help—not in the long run.'

'I know. It was a stupid idea—but that's me all over.'

'Don't put yourself down. You're not stupid. Anyone can make a mistake.'

'Tell me about it!' Sara laughed. Whoever this man was, he was the masterful kind, and she found herself responding despite her distrust of men.

They were outside the building. A short walk led them to Richard's car—an old Range Rover that looked a bit the worse for wear. He laughed as Sara hesitated.

'This is your car?'

'It's all right,' he said and grinned as she arched her brows. 'It goes better than it looks. I need something decent, but I haven't got around to buying anything yet. This is a loan from a farming friend. I've been abroad for a while, but I'm beginning to sort myself out.'

'It looks all right to me,' Sara said, feeling puzzled. It wasn't the condition of the vehicle that had made her ask if it was his. She had an idea that she'd seen his car parked outside St Saviour's recently, but was that likely? The hospital was miles away from this town, in a little Norfolk village a few miles from the seaside resort of Heacham. 'I was just wondering…' She shook her head. 'It doesn't matter.'

Richard opened the door for her. 'We'll find that coffee first,' he said. 'I know a pub near here that will serve us.'

Sara nodded but didn't answer. She didn't really need coffee. She'd drunk that gin and tonic quickly on an empty stomach but she was nowhere near as intoxicated as this man seemed to imagine. She wondered just who he was, wishing she could remember for certain where she'd seen his car parked. If it wasn't the small, country hospital where she worked, it must have been somewhere else that was important to her.

'What was making you so unhappy this evening?' he asked after a few minutes of driving in silence. 'Why were you with a man you obviously don't like?'

Sara shrugged her shoulders. 'Jonathan asked me to his party and I had to bring someone. I didn't expect Jeff to behave like that. I don't know him well. I just needed an escort—and he was looking for something I didn't want to give.'

'You don't have a regular partner?'

'No. To be honest, I'm not that keen on men at all.'

'Is there any particular reason why?'

Sara hesitated. She couldn't tell this stranger the truth.

'I've had a few bad experiences,' she said, her throat tight. 'I know you're not all like Jeff…but when you've been hurt…' Her voice faded away to a whisper. 'It was bad, really bad…I've never got over what happened. I was still in college…but that was a long time ago. I'm stupid to let it affect me. In fact, I'm not going to ever again. That's my New Year resolution. Scout's honour!'

'Do you want to talk?'

Sara shook her head. She hadn't been able to talk about that night to anyone, not even Julia, who was her closest friend. She found it too painful, and she felt foolish, too. Other girls went through similar experiences and carried on with their lives, so she was determined not to let it affect her—but sometimes the memory came back to haunt her.

'Sometimes it helps to talk,' Richard said. 'I'm a good listener and I don't make judgements. Pain festers inside you if you don't let it out.'

Sara glanced at him, noticing the tiny nerve flicking in his cheek as he struggled to retain his composure. 'You sound as if you've been there.'

'I know how it feels to be hurt.'

Sara wanted to tell him, it was there on the tip of her tongue, but she still couldn't let go of her fear. She changed the subject.

'Are you a friend of Jonathan's?'

'Yes. We go back a long way. Have you known him long?'

Sara shook her head. 'No, not really. He wants me to work for him at his clinic. I've always worked for the NHS, and I haven't been in my present job more than a few months.'

'Are you unhappy in your present work?'

'It's difficult… We've been so short-staffed recently…'

'If you leave, it will make things worse for them.'

'Yes, I know—that's part of the problem. I moved to this part of the country to make a new start, but nothing has changed…'

Richard was staring at her oddly.

'Is something the matter?' Sara asked.

'No, nothing,' he said, and frowned. 'Here's the pub I was talking about. We'll have that coffee then I'll drive you wherever you want to go.'

'I could stay with an aunt this evening,' Sara said. 'It's OK. I don't think I want coffee, thanks all the same. I don't really need to sober up. I was intending to get drunk at the party, but Jeff was way ahead of me.' She gave him an oddly shy, tentative look. 'You've helped me a lot this evening, Richard. I couldn't talk to my friends this way. They would think I was an idiot—and I am!'

She was a fool for letting something that had happened a long time ago still get to her. She ought to be strong enough to put all this out of her mind! But she had carried it with her for a long time, and was used to hiding the hurt.

Julia knew a part of Sara's story, but even she didn't know about that night. Besides, she worked in a big London teaching hospital and they didn't get to see each other much these days. Sometimes, when they both had a free weekend, they met and had fun together, but mostly they had to be content with phone calls. If Sara took a job in London… But that would make the problem worse. She had chosen to take the job at St Saviour's because she'd thought she would be able to put the past behind her—but the memories were still there in her head.

Richard stopped the car, then turned, his eyes intent on her face. His hand reached out, touching her long, light brown hair, letting it trail through his fingers. It was soft and silky, freshly washed.

'Don't put yourself down, Sara,' he said. 'I knew a girl like you once. She was pretty, too…but she didn't respect herself. She had no confidence in herself and she should have had, because she had a lot to live for…only she didn't know it.'

'What happened to her?' Sara was immediately alert. Was this girl the source of his own grief?

'She died,' Richard said, and the expression in his eyes was bleak. 'She took an overdose of painkillers and died slowly of liver failure. I watched her but could do nothing… It was a messy, terrible waste of life.' He ran his fingers down Sara's cheek. 'I wouldn't want to think something like that might happen to you. It isn't worth it, Sara. Believe me.'

'I believe you,' she said, feeling a twist of grief in her heart. It must be fate that they'd met this evening. His words had touched something deep within her. She felt a sense of relief, as though sharing this moment of intimacy with him had somehow released something inside her. How strange that they should both have experienced so much pain in their personal lives, though for very different reasons. 'I've seen it in my work. Young girls taking an overdose because they can't face up to their problems.'

She would never do that! She would never let anything drive her to take her own life. A few drinks at a party perhaps—but never an overdose of drugs.

She leaned towards him, her fresh light perfume, oddly sensual and wholly delicious, wafting towards him. Sara hesitated for a moment, then brushed her mouth against his in the softest of kisses.

'Thank you,' she said her throat catching, her voice husky. He seemed a nice, caring person, and just being with him had somehow helped to take away the bitter taste someone else had left in her mouth. 'You've been kind. Talking to you has helped.'

'I'm glad. If there's anything more I can do?'

'Just take me to my aunt's house. It wasn't fair of me to say I didn't have family. My Aunt Mary and Chris have been good to me. She lives just round the corner, then left again,' Sara said, smiling at him. The blackness of despair was easing from her mind, her natural resilience flowing back. 'I told her I might come tonight. That was before I decided to unburden my sorrows on my knight in shining armour.' Her soft laughter was infectious. She was suddenly a different girl, a girl who knew how to enjoy life. 'Please don't think I'm always like this. It was just one of my moods. They come and go. I was very tired but I feel fine now. Honestly.'

'Good.' Richard hesitated. He wondered if he ought to say something about wanting to meet her again, but decided against it. He was only just getting over Beth and he didn't want another involvement just yet. 'I hope things turn out better for you soon. You're sure to find the right man one of these days.'

Sara shook her head. 'No, I don't think so. I should only go and mess things up. I'm a walking disaster as far as men are concerned. You've been like the answer to a prayer this evening, Richard. I couldn't have talked this way if we hadn't been strangers. Most men don't want to listen to a girl they'll never see again. I just want to say thank you and goodbye.'

'Fine,' he said gently. 'I'll just fade into the background and you'll never see me again. Just like in the movies…'

'I'll never forget you,' she promised as he drew the car to a halt in front of her aunt's front door. 'You *were* my knight in shining armour, Richard. The way you stepped in and stopped Jeff hitting me was great. No one has ever done anything like that for me…and it's something I can remember for always.'

Richard smiled but didn't reply. He merely waved as she got out of the car and went to her aunt's front door, waiting until it was opened to admit her before driving away.

Sara sighed as she went in and closed the door behind her. It was funny how good it had felt, talking to Richard. She half regretted that he hadn't suggested meeting again, but she knew it wouldn't have worked. This way she had a good memory to hold on to when the bad ones came back to haunt her.

She'd tried to have a proper relationship, but it wasn't easy for her, and the few times she'd managed to get to the bedroom with a man she'd thought she liked enough, it had ended in disaster.

And that was down to two men—the medical student who had very nearly succeeded in raping her on their second date, and Peter Myers, her stepfather. She wasn't sure which of them she hated most. Simon had made her afraid to trust men when it came to the bedroom, but Peter had hurt her even more deeply, because of what he'd done to her mother. She would never forget that her much-loved mother had died in pain and distress because of him.

Mrs Myers had been dying of cancer. The doctors had offered her the painkillers that would have eased her last hours, but she'd refused them. She'd been waiting for Peter to come, waiting, hoping, enduring, and all in vain, because Peter hadn't arrived until it had been too late. And when he'd come at last, he'd smelt of whisky and a woman's strong, musky perfume.

Sara had known then that her mother's fears had been right. Her husband had been having an affair all the time Rose Myers had been ill with the cancer that had finally claimed her life.

Sara would never, never forgive him for what he'd done! She hated him, despised him—and had lost all faith in men because of him and Simon. But she thought she might have got over the shock and humiliation of that rape attempt if it hadn't been for the way her stepfather had hurt her mother. Because she hadn't loved Simon, but she had once loved Peter Myers very much, and that was what hurt so much—the betrayal of love.

She'd only half believed her mother when she'd first told Sara she thought her husband had someone else. Peter had always seemed to care for both his wife and his stepdaughter. Sara had believed in him until the proof of his faithlessness had been forced on her that terrible night. After her mother's death she hadn't been able to bear the sight of him. She'd screamed at him, accusing him of causing her mother's pain.

'She died in agony because of you,' she told him that night when her mother lay still and white in that hospital bed. 'I hate you, Peter. I never want to see you again.'

'It wasn't like that,' he protested. 'Give me a chance to explain…'

But Sara didn't give him a chance.

She accused him of wanting her mother to die so that he could inherit the large family house her mother had willed to him. Sara even went to a solicitor to try and have the will challenged, cutting him out completely, but the solicitor said there was nothing she could do.

After that, the persistent phone calls started, with Peter seemingly obsessed about trying to persuade Sara to talk with him. Driven to escape her painful memories, Sara moved away and changed her job, wanting to make a new life for herself.

She hoped that Peter would never find her—but he did.

He wrote to her, asking her if he could come and see her, asking again for the chance to explain.

So what did she do now? Sara lifted her head, anger and pride taking the place of the fear that had haunted her since his letter had arrived. She had moved once— but she was damned if she would do it again!

Let Peter do his worst. He had already ruined her life, there wasn't much more he could do to harm her.

Richard returned to the party after he'd dropped Sara off at her aunt's house. He'd arranged to stay at his friend's apartment for a few nights, and then at Jon's Norfolk cottage until he found himself a home and made up his mind what he wanted to do with his life.

He thought about Sara. On closer acquaintance, he'd realized she was neither as young nor as drunk as he'd first thought—just a mixed-up young woman.

He'd rescued Sara instinctively. As a boy, Richard had never been able to ignore a wounded bird or animal, and Sara's wounds had been bleeding openly as far as he was concerned. He had no doubt she was a very unhappy young woman, though instinct told him there was more to her story than she'd been prepared to tell him. After all, why should she confide completely in him?

The trouble was she reminded him of Beth, not in looks but because she was vulnerable and unhappy. Richard had been trying to forget the girl whose death still haunted his dreams at times. Since coming back to England and spending some time with his family, he'd begun to feel better. Christmas with Angela and the kids had helped a lot, but now the memories were threatening to overwhelm him. He thrust them away, found himself a glass of Jonathan's good wine and settled in a corner on his own, squatting on the floor beside a radiator. He still hadn't readjusted to this awful climate!

The year in Africa had been good for him, giving him time to do the soul-searching he'd needed, to sort out his feelings about himself and the world in general. He was no longer driven, just saddened by his memories, which he'd begun to think would overshadow him for the rest of his life.

A car crash on a lonely road, where he'd narrowly missed being burnt alive, had made him realize it had been time to think about what he wanted to do with the rest of his life. He'd come back to England and taken a job that he was over-qualified for because he needed time to think, to work out where he was going and why. The last thing he needed right now was to get involved with a vulnerable woman. Yet he couldn't get Sara out of his mind. Just why had she been so unhappy?

His thoughts were yanked back to the present as Jonathan came to squat beside him on the carpet.

'I thought you left?'

'I took Sara to her aunt's home, that's all.'

Jonathan nodded. 'Silly girl. I don't know what got into her this evening. I was thinking of offering her a job at the clinic—but if she has a drink problem...'

'No, I don't think she has. I thought she was an unhappy girl this evening, but she wasn't drunk.'

Jonathan looked thoughtful, then nodded. 'Yes, you may be right. She's a bit of a mystery, never talks about her past. I took her out a couple of times...tried it on, the way you do...'

'And? What happened?' Richard was interested.

'She put me off. Made out she really wanted to but it was the wrong time...you know. Said she was sorry and maybe next time...'

'Maybe she just didn't fancy you.' Richard smiled at him with affection. 'Strange as it may seem, women are entitled to say no.'

'Right!' Jonathan grinned good-naturedly. 'But I got the feeling she was scared—and you know me, Rich. I'm not a tiger. I'm a pussy-cat. Push me and I roll over and beg.'

'I know it,' Richard said. 'So if she doesn't want men to try it on, why does she give out the wrong signals? That silver dress was a come-on if ever I saw one. And yet she does seem to have some kind of a hang-up about men—I wonder why?'

It was odd that a woman as sexy and appealing to men as Sara Linden should be so wary—unless someone had hurt her that way? She'd hinted at something to him in the car but then had drawn back, as if she hadn't quite been able to bring herself to tell him. The thought that a man had hurt her made Richard angry. Some men were bastards! Sara didn't deserve to be treated that way, even if she did wear skimpy dresses that left little to the imagination.

Richard found her intriguing, and that slightly haunted look in her eyes had touched something deep inside him. A woman like that needed someone to protect her. He laughed inwardly as he realized where his thoughts were leading him. No way! The last thing he needed was to get involved with Sara Linden! He'd been through one traumatic experience. He didn't need another.

'Who understands what any woman thinks?' Jonathan said ruefully. 'I gave up trying ages ago. Now I just do as I'm told. Helen is a very determined woman. All I have to do is agree with her and everything is fine.'

Richard laughed but made no comment. His friend's

partner was inclined to boss him around, but he seemed to thrive on it.

It was good being with Jonathan again; it felt like old times, when they'd been students together. Before he'd gone to New York...before Beth.

'So...' Jonathan was saying. 'What about coming in with us, Rich?'

'Give me a few weeks,' Richard said. 'I've promised to do this locum job for Jack Harper. He's my brother-in-law, in case you'd forgotten, and he's been run off his feet recently. Angela says if he doesn't have some evenings off soon, she's going to divorce him. She doesn't mean it, but he looks shattered. I've registered with the powers that be for temporary work for the time being. They were a little sniffy about me being over-qualified for general practice, but I managed to convince them that I haven't any dire secrets that ought to get me banned from ever practising medicine again. And it's only as a favour to Jack. He is going to advertise for a new partner, and hopefully that won't take too long. By then I'll have a clearer picture of what I want to do.'

In a few weeks the bad dreams might have gone—they were already becoming less frequent. Given time, Richard might be able to get a decent night's sleep again. That was if he didn't dwell too much on another vulnerable young woman who ought to have had more sense than to get involved with unsuitable men.

CHAPTER TWO

SARA was concentrating on the shopping list her aunt had given her. She ticked most of it off in her mind, then saw the last item—kitchen rolls. Yes, she'd known there was something else. She paused at the edge of the pavement, waiting for a lull in the traffic, then dashed across the road. As she turned to her right, she stopped, her heart catching as she saw him.

Richard Dalton was looking at some shirts in the window of a shop at the corner of the street. He hadn't noticed her. She could turn away, avoid him, and he would never know. Yet that would be foolish. Surely there was no need to be so extreme? She'd made a bit of a fool of herself the other evening, but Richard had helped her and, if she were honest, she'd thought about him more than she'd expected during her three days of holiday.

Sara laughed at her own hesitation, went up to him and touched his arm. He turned and looked surprised when he saw her. She'd been shopping in the sales, and was loaded with carrier bags.

'Hi,' she said, her smile warm and friendly. What are you doing in town this morning?'

'The same as you,' Richard replied, treating her to the lazy grin she'd begun to find very appealing. 'Judging by those carrier bags, it looks as if you've been more successful than me.'

Sara was aware of interest in his slate-grey eyes as they went over her. She was wearing jeans and a warm yellow ski jacket, her long hair tied up in a ponytail. With her face scrubbed clean of the heavy make-up she'd worn on New Year's Eve, she looked about eighteen, though she was actually twenty-six.

However, she seldom paid much attention to her own appearance, and it was the last thing on her mind just now. *His* was far more interesting. He was wearing black jeans, a black roll-neck sweater and a heavy wool jacket that was looking decidedly the worse for wear. His hair was definitely in need of a trim, though she rather liked the way it seemed to curl at the nape of his neck.

'You're not taking it seriously enough,' Sara said, giving him a teasing look. She was over her black mood of the other evening, and had been enjoying herself buying new clothes. 'What do you need?'

'Everything,' Richard replied, pulling a rueful face. 'I lost all my gear in a fire a few months back. What I'm wearing now belongs to someone else.'

'This doesn't look like your sort of shop,' Sara said, a twinkle in her eyes. 'There are a couple of trendy boutiques round the corner—designer stuff. Great if you can afford it. One of them has a sale on now. You might find a bargain there if you're quick. I saw some snazzy combat trousers that would look good on you. Some men look awful in them, but you've got the right build for them.'

'Thanks.' Richard was grateful for the information. He hadn't been shopping for clothes in England for years and wasn't aware that the shops selling designer gear were there. 'I don't really like new clothes at all, and I detest shopping for them—but I have to buy some.'

Sara nodded, preparing to walk on. 'Well, it was nice seeing you, Richard…'

'Do you have to go? We could have coffee somewhere.'

'I need to get these things back to the house,' she said.

'I'm catching a train at two o'clock. I'm on duty later this evening. I've had four days' holiday, but now it's back to the wards.'

'Fair enough,' Richard replied. 'Maybe we'll bump into each other again soon.'

'Maybe it's fate,' Sara replied with a teasing smile. 'Maybe we're meant to know one another…'

It was very odd, but she was almost hoping they would get to know each other better.

'Stranger things have happened.' Richard smiled. She seemed different this morning, a much more balanced, friendly person. Whatever had upset her on New Year's Eve, she seemed to have come to terms with it now. 'Be seeing you, Sara.'

He watched as she walked away, then turned and headed towards the shops she'd mentioned. He needed to buy something suitable for work, but a good pair of jeans, some shirts and sweaters were top of his list.

He found his thoughts straying to the woman he'd just met for the second time. Had Sara been buying more of those sexy dresses? She looked really pretty this morning. He wondered why she thought it necessary to smother her face in make-up when she went out at night. She certainly didn't need it…unless it was some sort of talisman?

She was certainly very attractive—and sexy. He wondered about what Jonathan had told him concerning her. He would have expected a woman as attractive as Sara to have a settled partner, or at least to have had several love affairs behind her, but according to Jonathan she didn't have anyone special and wasn't into sleeping around. Besides, she'd made that fact plain to him from the start.

Of course he wasn't interested in an affair himself.

It was going to take him a long time to get over Beth. If he'd only been less impatient...less critical! Beth had needed understanding and love. Why hadn't he realized it at the time? Why hadn't he known she'd been so unhappy?

He would have given anything to go back and try again. But it was too late. Beth's cry for help had gone unheeded, and now she was dead. All the regret, all the self-blame wouldn't bring her back again.

No, Richard wasn't interested in having an affair—but it didn't stop him being curious about Sister Sara Linden...

Back in Norfolk at the house she shared with friends, Sara wondered about stopping off to talk with Angela Harper, but decided she didn't have time. Her train had been twenty minutes late and then her car had had a fit of the sulks after being left out over the new year. If she didn't hurry, she would be late for work. Perhaps if she had time, she might call on Angela the next day and take the children some sweets she'd brought back with her, presents she had no intention of eating from well meaning friends. Why did everyone always try to fatten her up?

Drawing her rather battered but much beloved Austin Mini Cooper to a stop in front of the hospital, Sara put all thoughts of anything other than work from her mind as she went up in the lifts to her wards, which were on the top floor of the small hospital.

St Saviour's was a pleasant and modern, well-equipped hospital, though smaller than Sara had been used to before she'd come here. All the doctors and nurses here were on good terms, and there was a vibrant social club going, which helped morale in a village that had very little entertainment otherwise.

At the moment she was in charge of G2, G3 and G4, which were geriatric wards, and always busy, particularly at this time of the year. Winter was a bad time for older people, because coughs and colds so often turned to rather nasty chest infections, and, of course, there were always the stroke cases, which often accounted for more than half her patients.

'Hi, there,' Staff Nurse Gillian Smith said as she arrived at her office at the corner of G3 and G4. 'How was your holiday?'

'OK,' Sara said. 'My aunt was pleased to see me— and so was Chris. He's got a new motorbike, and we took the bikes out for a spin yesterday.'

'Rather you than me,' Gillian said. 'I don't know how you dare ride one of those things. I couldn't even ride pillion.'

'It's just something you either enjoy or you don't,' Sara said. 'Chris was always a big fan, so I suppose I went along with him...'

Her cousin Chris had been a good friend after her mother had died. He was about three years younger than her and Sara wasn't sure what she would have done if she hadn't had his shoulder to cry on at times.

Thinking of a shoulder to cry on made Sara remember Richard Dalton. She'd been thinking about him all the way down on the train. Not that there was much point in regretting her refusal to have coffee with him. They weren't likely to meet again.

She blocked the thought out, then picked up the notes left for her by Day Sister. It seemed they'd had two stroke victims in earlier that day, one of whom was particularly ill and needed watching. There was also an el-

derly man with a broken hip, who'd been brought up to
the ward after having surgery that morning and was making a good recovery. One of her favourites was a man in
his seventies, who'd come in for a gall bladder operation,
then developed pneumonia. He was still with them but
doing so well he was going to be released in a day or so
after a visit from his own GP, who would be responsible
for keeping an eye on him at home.

She nodded to Gillian. 'I'll just check on Mr Ross,
then I'll do the round as usual. Carry on with whatever
you were doing before I arrived.'

'I was about ton give Mrs Ryder in G3 a bed bath,'
Gillian said. 'The poor dear had her op three days ago
and she really wants a proper bath, but she isn't up to it
yet and she's feeling a bit low so I thought I would just
make her feel a little fresher. That sometimes helps more
than all the pills...'

'Ah, yes, I remember her.'

Sara nodded. She had seen the name in the notes for
G3. Mrs Ryder was seventy-three and had had an emergency operation for appendicitis, which had been made
worse because of her age. It was hardly surprising she
couldn't manage to go to the bathroom just yet.

A junior nurse or an auxiliary usually gave bed baths,
but once again they were short-staffed, this time mainly
because of a flu bug that had been going the rounds since
just before the holidays. This evening, it seemed that
Gillian and Sara were the only two to have turned up out
of a staff of five—which was hardly enough even then.
It could turn out to be a busy night!

'Yes, you do that,' Sara said. 'I can imagine how Mrs
Ryder feels—and the day staff don't always have enough
time to get round to everyone, not the way things are at
the moment. If anything, they are busier than we are.'

'We ought to have some agency nurses in to make up the shortfall,' Gillian said. 'But I suppose there's not much chance of that, is there?'

'Not at the moment. I think we're running over budget already,' Sara said, pulling a face. 'So—instead of standing here talking, we'd better get on.'

Gillian grinned at her and pushed her trolley out into the corridor. Sara sighed. No matter how awkward things were for her privately, she never had time to worry once she got to work.

The problems they were facing at St Saviour's at the moment made it all the more necessary that she shouldn't let her stepfather drive her away. Besides, she felt she still owed something to the NHS. A lot of nurses had become fed up with the hours and low pay, but Sara was resisting the move to private health care for the moment.

Picking up her clipboard, she checked her watch and went into G4 to begin her first round of the evening. For a moment her mind veered back to Richard Dalton, then she firmly pushed all such thoughts away.

She stopped by Mr Ross's bed and smiled at him. 'How are you today? A little bird whispered to me that you might be going home soon.'

'In time for my granddaughter's eighteenth birthday party,' he said. 'I do hope so, Sister Linden. She was in to see me over the weekend, and so excited. I want to be there if I can.'

'Well, talk to your GP when he comes in, Mr Ross. You'll need someone to keep an eye on you at home, but I'm sure he'll be happy to call on you until you're more mobile.'

'You're such a caring woman,' the old man said. 'I shall miss you when they do send me home.'

Sara laughed and shook her head. 'You'll be much too

busy getting ready for that party to think about me.' She glanced at her notes. 'I see you've had a little trouble with your bowels. We'll give you something this evening—but make sure your own doctor keeps an eye on the problem.'

She smiled at him again and moved on to the next patient. Mr Ross was lucky in having a loving family to go home to. Unfortunately, not all her patients were so fortunate. Some of them were well enough to leave hospital, but they had nowhere to go.

'Leave Uncle Richard in peace,' Angela Harper said to her children as they climbed all over him on his arrival the following afternoon. 'He has to work later.'

'I'm shaking in my boots,' Richard said, grinning at her. 'Jack is a hard act to follow.'

'Yes, he is,' Angela replied seriously. She was a pretty woman, slim and energetic, which she needed to be to keep up with her three children, all of them under nine. 'You won't find it easy, Richard. I don't doubt your ability as a doctor, but Jack gives so much more. His patients think the world of him.'

'Yes. I'd gathered that,' Richard replied. 'I'm going down to the surgery later to meet Jack's partners.'

'They're fine,' Angela said. 'But Andrew is a bit of a bore sometimes. He won't think much to that car of yours, Rich. If you're short of money, I think we could probably lend you some…'

'No, thanks, Angela. It took a while for the transfer to come through, but the money I was waiting for arrived from New York a couple of days ago. I still have to sell my apartment out there, but I'm in no hurry. I have enough to see me through. I'm not exactly on the breadline, even though I haven't been working for a while.'

'No, I should hope not,' Angela said, looking pleased by his confirmation. 'You know you can move in here for a while if you want?'

'I knew you'd offer,' Richard said, 'but the cottage Jonathan lent me is fine for the moment. He only uses it for weekends in the summer, and I'll be gone long before then. I tend to prowl at night—besides, if I'm on call-out the telephone could disturb you and the kids.'

'All right.' Angela smiled at him wickedly. 'I wouldn't want to cramp your style.'

Richard laughed. He didn't bother to deny her suggestion that there might be another reason he wanted his own place, though there was no chance of him starting a love affair. His sister was like a terrier. Once she knew he'd been engaged to a girl who'd died, she wouldn't let go until he told her every last detail—and that was still too painful.

His first harsh grief had faded somewhere along the line, but the regrets lingered.

Leaving his sister to the washing-up she insisted was no problem, Richard drove the short distance to her husband's surgery. His thoughts turning once more to the woman who was occupying them far more than his brief acquaintance with her merited. With an effort, he put Sara out of his mind, and thought about the set-up here.

Richard was accustomed to working in large, busy, very modern hospitals with all the latest technology at his fingertips. Passing St Saviour's, he thought it seemed small and old-fashioned. He supposed it had its place as somewhere for patients to convalesce after an operation, and Jack had told him the geriatric wards were better than most. They weren't equipped for major surgery, but he knew minor routine operations were sometimes carried out here and Jack thought the A and E unit was excellent.

Which was just as well if they had to send their patients there in an emergency. It was a long way to the
nearest large NHS hospital, which was at King's Lynn.

He parked his disreputable vehicle in Jack's reserved
space in front of the surgery, feeling rather like an im-
postor. He had completed his basic training at a large
teaching hospital, and his qualifications were, of course,
the equal of his brother-in-law's. Had he wished, he
could have become a GP, his original intention, but at
the last moment he'd discovered that he'd wanted to go
on with his training and become a surgeon.

His years of experience and intensive training in
America entitled him to the rank of Surgical Consultant,
but he'd left all that behind him when he'd packed his
bags and fled New York. After Beth's tragic death, he'd
abandoned all that he'd known and been.

Here in this tiny village, he was simply Dr Richard
Dalton, a pale substitute for his popular brother-in-law.
It was a humbling thought. Mr Richard Dalton, the brilliant reconstructive surgeon, was merely a memory. He
felt almost as nervous as he had during his first days on
the wards as a junior houseman.

He gritted his teeth and went into the surgery. Time to
meet Jack's partners and be briefed. He already knew it
was a very busy practice, which covered this village and
another a few miles away. His part for the next few
weeks was to be on night call, standing in for Jack who,
being younger than his partners, had borne the brunt of
the call-outs up to now and was due for a well-earned
rest.

Richard visited Mr Ross on the geriatric ward up at St
Saviour's that evening. The elderly man was very alert
and eager to go home, seeming to have made a speedy

recovery from the pneumonia which had followed his operation.

'My brother-in-law asked me to call this evening. Dr Harper will be away for a few days,' Richard said. 'I'm taking his place for a while. He's asked me to keep an eye on you. I think we can arrange transport home tomorrow morning, and I shall call on you at home tomorrow afternoon, to make sure you are settling in.'

'I shall be glad to get back to my Annie, Doctor.' Mr Ross frowned. 'She can't manage to remember her tablets if I'm not there. The family are very good, but they can't be watching out for her all the time.'

'What does she suffer from?' Richard asked.

'It's her heart, Doctor. I try to look after her—but I'm the invalid now. Still, I shall be better once I get home.'

'Don't try to do too much at first, Mr Ross. We shall provide home visits from the nurse and myself for a while—but don't forget, the surgery is there for your benefit. Any of us will be pleased to help you in any way we can.'

'That's what Dr Harper always says,' the elderly man said, nodding. 'Follow in his footsteps, young man, and you won't go far wrong.'

'I shall certainly do my best,' Richard replied, and went away chuckling to himself. It was a far cry from the days when junior doctors had fluttered round him as he'd carried out delicate and skilful operations, but it was a good way of getting back to work—and he felt it was a price he needed to pay. Besides, he needed to keep busy and he wasn't sure yet that he could go back to surgery. His gift had been very special, and there was a possibility that he would find he was no longer able to perform to the high standards he had always set himself.

He left the ward, still smiling inwardly. He was sure

Jack's patient still only half believed he was qualified to take over from his regular GP.

'Hello.' A male voice accosted him from behind. 'You're Richard Dalton, aren't you? Jack Harper's brother-in-law?'

'Yes.' Richard waited for the white-coated doctor to catch up to him. 'Sorry. I don't believe we've met.'

'David Lanigan. Jack and I play golf together some-times—are you a player?'

'Sorry.' Richard shook his head. 'I'm a rugby man. I've been playing American football for the past five years, just as an amateur on the hospital team—but no golf.'

'Oh, well, it can't be helped. Thought you might like a game some time—we've got quite a good course near by.' The doctor smiled. He was a man of about forty-five, greying hair, distinguished-looking. 'Got time for a coffee in the canteen? You might like to meet a few members of staff. I believe you're on the agency list for temporary work. Jack said you might help us out if we were short-staffed.'

'Be pleased to when I'm not on call for the surgery. I'm standing in for Jack full time at the moment, but that's only for a few days. After that I'm on night call-outs until they find their new partner.'

'Any idea of what you want to do in the future?' Lanigan asked as they made their way to the canteen. 'I ask because we're going to need an extra surgeon here once we get the new theatre unit up and running. Our present one is a bit outdated. We tackle emergencies or small routine stuff at the moment. We can do with the new unit, but these things take time. Won't be for a year, come to think of it.'

'I expect to be working by then,' Richard said. 'Besides, my field isn't general surgery. I did consider it at one time, but I was offered the chance to work in plastic surgery and I took it.'

'Cosmetic stuff,' Lanigan said, nodding. 'Pays well, so I hear.'

'Yes, it does,' Richard admitted. 'But it isn't just lifting double chins and giving patients straight noses. Accident victims sometimes need their faces rebuilt, and people with terrible facial burns can be helped a great deal by plastic surgery these days.'

'Yes, of course. It's just that one always thinks of the glamour side of things.'

'That doesn't interest me much, though I've done my share. I worked mainly with trauma victims—cancer, too. We often find that we need to reconstruct someone's features completely after a cancer has been removed. Without the skill of a good surgeon, that patient would never be able to live in the world again with any confidence.'

'No...' Lanigan was struck by the sombre truth. 'You're quite right. That side of your work tends to get overlooked. I'm sorry if I sounded condescending just now.'

'Don't apologize,' Richard said. 'Most people think the way you do, until something happens to people they know and love. Very few realize just how much we can do these days.'

They had now reached the canteen. Several heads turned curiously as they walked in. David Lanigan made his announcement in a general way.

'Hey, everyone, this is Richard Dalton. He's Jack Harper's brother-in-law and standing in for him while Jack has a rest.'

There was a murmur of greeting, smiles and acknowledgement. Across the room, Richard became aware of a woman's shocked face. Their eyes met for a moment, and then she turned and left the room abruptly, leaving her coffee untouched on the counter.

Richard swore beneath his breath. He might have guessed the hospital where Sara worked was likely to have been St Saviour's. He had seen disbelief and then anger in her eyes, and he didn't blame her. He ought to have told her more about what he was up to to save this embarrassment between them.

He hadn't realized she'd been there until she'd turned, and by then it had been too late. Lanigan had already made his announcement.

'Sorry,' he muttered. 'I've just remembered something. I'll take a rain check on the coffee.'

He turned and strode swiftly from the canteen. Sara was just disappearing round the corner of the long corridor. He went after her, calling her name. She was still walking when he turned the corner. He called to her again, but she didn't stop or look round. He ran after her, catching at her arm, forcing her to stop and look at him.

'Sara. What's the matter?'

She looked at him then, her eyes glittering. 'How could you embarrass me like that? You might have let me know you were coming down here. I feel such a fool…'

'I honestly didn't make the connection as there are a few other hospitals in the area.' He frowned. 'I don't really see what all the fuss is about.'

'Don't you?' she said. 'If I'd known we'd be likely to keep running in to each other, I'd not have told you the things I did about myself. If you've said anything to Dr Lanigan…'

Richard's eyes darkened with anger. 'As far as I recall, you told me very little. Nothing of substance that I could reveal to your friends—and let me tell you, I find the suggestion that I might insulting. I'm not in the habit of spreading gossip.'

Sara flushed, knowing she'd been rude. 'Why didn't you tell me you were coming here?'

'At first I didn't think it was relevant,' he said honestly. 'I see now that I should have mentioned the possibility that we might meet up again, and if I've upset you I'm sorry.'

She nodded, realizing that she owed him an apology. 'Thank you. I'm sorry I blew my top. It was just the shock of seeing you there.'

'Well, you won't be seeing me here that often,' Richard said, 'but I shall be around so you'd better be prepared for it.'

With that he turned and walked off, leaving Sara to stare after him.

Sara gathered her composure before going to talk to Mrs Reed. The patient had been admitted earlier in the day, but as yet no one had explained to her just what had gone wrong with her diabetes. Until now, she'd been on tablets and managing quite well, but her condition had suddenly become much worse after an illness which had required her to take steroids, and she would be needing insulin from now on. It was bound to be a shock to her, but she was a sensible woman and would, no doubt, learn to cope with her new routine.

'I knew things were going wrong,' Mrs Reed said after Sara had explained what had happened. 'I've always managed to keep my sugar at a reasonable level, but recently it has been going haywire. I suppose I should have gone to the doctor sooner.'

Sara was sitting on the edge of her bed. She reached out and took her patient's hand, feeling it tremble. Mrs

Reed had been very ill when she'd been brought in, close to dehydration and vomiting constantly. It must have been a frightening experience for her, especially as she'd already been aware of the dangers from her diabetes being out of control.

'Your doctor had explained that the steroids tablets you were taking for your blood condition could make your sugar more difficult to control, I suppose?'

'Yes, he was very good,' Anne Reed said. 'But it was Christmas and the family were staying. I thought I could manage.'

'It was unfortunate,' Sara said, taking care to use layman's terms and not confuse the elderly lady with medical ones. 'You do understand that without the steroids you might have gone blind, don't you? They are very necessary to control the pressure behind your eyes. It isn't something we can just stop because your diabetes is affected. You will have to take them for a long time—perhaps for the rest of your life. We know that there are sometimes complications or side effects with this type of medicine, particularly when it has to be taken orally, but you can't manage without it, I'm afraid.'

'Which means I'm going to be on insulin, doesn't it?'

'Yes, I'm afraid it does,' Sara said. 'But don't be frightened by that, Anne. We'll teach you how to do the injections, and before you go home you'll have become adjusted to the new regime. That's why you have to stay here for a while, because we need to ascertain the level of insulin you need. It isn't quite the same as taking tablets. You have to learn to balance it properly.'

'Yes, I know.' Anne Reed smiled at her. 'I've read all about it in the diabetic magazine, Sister. I take it regularly. There's a lot of little things they tell you that help when you've got diabetes—even the kind I had before this.'

'Good. I'm glad you can contemplate the change without too much distress.'

'There's not much point doing anything else, is there? We all have our troubles, don't we, Sister Linden? I'm lucky it isn't any worse.'

Sara smiled and nodded. The bravery of some of her patients astounded her at times.

At least this evening they had four of their five staff available, Sara thought as she made her rounds, checking patients' notes at the foot of each bed, writing up their details and making comments where necessary.

This second part of the evening was always her favourite. The medicine trolley had been round, the pills dispensed. Now it was just a matter of checking that the patients were comfortable—unless a new case was brought in. Which was happening now.

Sara increased her pace as she saw the bed being wheeled in by one of the nurses from A and E. She gave a little cry of distress as she saw it was Mrs Margaret Philips. She had been released only three days previously after a stay of some weeks, but it was obvious that she'd had another stroke—and this time it looked much worse than the last one.

Sara hurried to the nurse who was bringing the patient in, asking questions as a space was made near the door where it would be easier to keep an eye on the new arrival.

'Why wasn't I told you were bringing this patient up?'

'Someone rang through,' the nurse said, just as Gillian Smith came hurrying up.

'Sorry, Sister,' she apologized. 'You were talking to Mrs Reed when the call came. I was going to tell you when you'd finished—but then I had an emergency call for a bedpan.'

Sara nodded. She would have preferred to have been told immediately, but understood the nurse's dilemma.

Sara sighed as she went out to her car the next morning. It was covered by a white frost and the engine moaned and groaned before coming reluctantly to life. She felt like groaning herself. It had been a heavy night, with four emergency admissions and one death.

Margaret Philips had died just before dawn despite all they could do for her. It made Sara's tiredness seem worse. She always hated it when they lost a patient like that, but there was nothing they could have done. The stroke had been massive and fatal, and the elderly lady would most likely have been severely paralysed if she'd recovered consciousness. So perhaps it had been best that way—but she'd only been somewhere around seventy, not that old by today's standards.

Perhaps she ought to think of asking for a transfer to a more lively ward. Sara thought about it and then laughed. Her patients often kept her amused with their jokes, and their cheerfulness in the face of what they often had to endure was nothing short of amazing. The death of a patient was always hard to take, especially one as likeable as Mrs Philips. Sara felt a real affection for her patients; most of them were so friendly, so easy to please. A few were cantankerous, of course, but that was only to be expected.

No, she wouldn't ask for a transfer. Besides, it wasn't just the death that was getting to her. The way Richard Dalton had turned up so unexpectedly the previous day—and his obvious irritation with her impulsive behaviour—had been playing on her mind.

She'd made a fool of herself, running away like that! He would think she was neurotic or something and steer clear of her in future. Sara wasn't sure why that made her feel so low. She didn't really want to go out with the handsome doctor—did she?

It was true that her heart had a habit of behaving oddly when he was around, but that didn't mean she was willing to take a risk on him. She'd made too many mistakes in that department, so many that the only safe course seemed to stay clear of dating.

No, no, it would only end the same way if she did. After a few dates he would expect their relationship to move on—and she would think she could go through with it, then her memories would come back to haunt her. It had happened so many times. She couldn't seem to trust anyone when it got to the bedroom.

It wasn't that she hated sex. Before her unpleasant experience with Simon she'd one brief but quite pleasant affair with a friend of Chris's. They'd gone steady for a few months, then parted on mutual terms of agreement, because Ken had wanted to concentrate on his studies and she'd always known their affair hadn't been going anywhere. She'd liked but not loved him. Then Simon had tried to rape her. It had been an ugly, painful experience and Sara had been left with a load of anger mixed with guilt. Simon had said it had been her fault, that she'd led him on—but that just wasn't true. She knew it wasn't and yet still felt guilty.

After that Sara had begun to distrust men and this had been compounded by the trauma of her mother's death. Even the ones you loved and thought loved you let you down. Maybe it was her fault that her relationships went wrong, but they had left her with a nasty taste in the mouth and a reluctance to believe in any man.

At least that was how she'd felt until she'd met Richard Dalton. Since then she'd been doing some serious soul-searching. Sara wasn't sure how she really felt about anything any more. Was she really preparing to spend the rest of her life alone?

She hadn't been able to put Richard Dalton out of her mind. She'd been instinctively drawn to him, inclined to trust him. Yet she knew next to nothing about him. Just who was he and what had brought him to a remote village like this?

CHAPTER THREE

'MR ARNOLD, isn't it?' Richard shook hands with the forty-five-year-old man who had just entered the consulting room. 'I've been reading your notes. I understand Dr Harper sent you for an endoscopy two months ago—how may I help?'

'I saw a consultant at the hospital yesterday,' Mr Arnold said, frowning. 'It was really just a chat I wanted…to clear my mind. That consultant, he said I ought to have an operation for a hiatus hernia, said my condition wouldn't respond well to the usual treatment. I didn't quite follow him. Dr Harper said I would probably need to take tablets, but he didn't think they would operate.'

'That's because we weren't sure how bad your condition was,' Richard said, glancing at the detailed notes Jack had made. 'Sometimes the reflux can be controlled by taking cimetidine, which is what you've been given, but in your case the endoscopy revealed chronic irritation of the oesophagus lining.'

'Does that mean I've got to have the op?' Mr Arnold frowned. 'I know someone who has had a hernia for years. He hasn't had an operation, and he's all right.'

'You have something that we call GORD, which is short for gastro-oesophageal reflux disease,' Richard explained. 'It makes your condition a little more serious. It could lead to unpleasant complications like oesophagitis, which is a chronic irritation of the lining of the oesophagus, if left untreated.'

45

'Is the op dangerous?'

'Any operation carries a risk,' Richard said. 'In your case, the surgeon will narrow the hiatus by inserting non-absorbable sutures around the opening. It's a fairly straightforward procedure, and I would advise you to have the surgery carried out rather than leave it and perhaps risk a more serious condition in the future. In chronic cases of GORD there's a risk of cancer developing if it's neglected.'

'Ah, I see,' Mr Arnold said and nodded. 'Thank you for explaining in layman's terms. I didn't take it all in yesterday. Bit of a shock.'

'No one likes having surgery,' Richard said. 'I saw this operation done many times when I was training, Mr Arnold. It's normally very successful, and we rarely see complications. Your heart is good and you're perfectly healthy in other ways. You should be fine.'

'Good. Well, I'd better go ahead with it, then. Will you let the consultant know I've decided to have the operation? I told him yesterday that I needed to think about it.'

'Yes, of course. We'll arrange it for you. You'll receive your details through the post. It may not be for a few months. Your condition isn't considered urgent, though the operation is very necessary for your future health.'

'I'll wait to hear, then.' Mr Arnold stood up. 'Thank you for your time.'

'My pleasure. Goodbye.'

Richard made some notes on the computer, then glanced at his watch. It was just seven-thirty. His list hadn't been particularly heavy, but that was good because he'd been able to spend time going through patients' histories, and talking them through their symptoms.

He left the practice feeling pleased with the experience of his first surgery standing in for Jack, who was away for a short break with Angela.

It hadn't been too bad, although, as he'd expected, some patients had been disappointed at not finding Jack in his room. Most had accepted Richard without question, but one elderly lady had been upset when he'd changed her tablets. He'd explained that the medication was an improvement, but she had looked doubtful until he told her that Jack had left instructions for the change.

'Oh… Well, I suppose it's all right, then.'

'I'm sure you'll find them much better, Mrs Saunders.'

Richard hid his amusement as she went out. In America, his reputation had meant that he'd lived in a slightly rarefied atmosphere. Beth had once told him that he enjoyed playing God—that had been when she'd been in one of her dark moods. She'd cried afterwards, begging him to forgive her. She'd been such a vulnerable girl, and he hadn't always been as understanding as he ought. Lack of time hadn't been an excuse—he should have made time to listen to her more often.

He frowned as he got into his car and drove back to the cottage. He had been invited out for a meal that evening, but he wasn't really in the mood. Perhaps he would phone and cancel, though the alternative of staying in alone didn't particularly appeal either.

For a moment he found himself thinking about Sara Linden. She was attractive and she intrigued him, but he would be a fool to get involved with her.

His reverie was interrupted by the noise of two motorbikes coming up behind him fast. They seemed to be having a race, and he was swiftly overtaken by both. The speed they were going at was much too fast for country roads and he felt a flicker of annoyance. The idiots! Didn't they know what they were risking?

It was so foolish to tempt fate. The results of an accident on a motorbike could be devastating. Richard had patched up too many road accident victims to feel tolerant of such behaviour.

He wasn't really surprised when he turned a bend and saw that one of the bikes had skidded across the road into a dike. The other rider had stopped and was looking round as if seeking help.

Richard pulled over to the kerb and got out.

'Is anyone hurt?' he asked. 'I'm a doctor.'

Even as he spoke, the rider who had come off came stumbling up the side of the ditch, apparently unhurt apart from a tear in his leathers. He was small and slight, and looked extremely thin in the tight-fitting leathers.

'Damned young fools!' Richard said curtly, feeling relieved. 'Don't you know you could have killed yourselves? These roads aren't meant for speeding.'

The rider who had fallen took off his protective helmet. Long straight brown hair came tumbling down onto...*her* shoulders. It was a girl, and a girl he knew! For a moment Richard stared, hardly able to believe his eyes. Surely he was mistaken?

'Sara!' he exclaimed. 'What on earth did you think you were doing?'

Her face looked white in the light of his headlamps. She looked extremely vulnerable, obviously shaken and distressed.

'Are you all right?' Richard demanded, suddenly furious with her, though he didn't know why. 'Have you hurt yourself?'

'No...I was lucky.' Her voice was husky. She looked

close to tears but was fighting them. 'I'm sorry, Chris. I think the bike is damaged.'

'Not your fault. I swerved in front of you.'

'You had to,' Sara said. 'The dog…'

She gave a little sigh and suddenly started to crumple. Richard moved quickly and caught her before she could fall, lowering her carefully to the ground.

'What's the matter?' Chris demanded. He looked worried. 'It's my fault. I swerved to avoid a dog that ran into the road and she braked too hard. I should've hit that damned thing!'

Richard was bending over her, searching for signs of injury. He felt her neck and head carefully but found nothing to alarm him.

'Is she all right?' Chris asked.

'I think so, but I'll ring for an ambulance just in case.'

'No! Don't make a fuss.' Sara had her eyes open and was looking up at him. 'I'm OK. I just fainted. I'm not hurt.'

'You don't know that. You should check in at A and E just to be sure.'

'I didn't even bang my head, I just slid across the road,' Sara said. 'It's all right, Richard. Honestly. I'll probably have a few bruises, but I'm fine. It isn't the first time I've come off a bike.'

'She rides motor-cross,' Chris said. 'She's a damned good rider, too.'

'And who are you?' Richard asked coldly. His eyes had the sharpness of honed steel. 'What do you mean by allowing Sara to ride like that on the road? You were both exceeding the speed limit. I ought to report you both.'

'Please, don't,' Sara said, laying her hand on his arm. 'We were just having fun.'

'The sort of fun that could have killed you!'

'I know. I'm sorry. We were trying out Chris's new bike—he's my cousin.' Sara gave him a look of appeal. 'Please, don't report us, Richard. He could lose his licence, and he has several big races coming up soon. It would ruin everything for him—for us both.'

'I said I *ought* to, for your own sakes.' Richard glared at her. 'That doesn't mean I'm going to. I'll make a deal with you—let me take you up to A and E and I'll let this go.' He sounded as though he meant it.

Sara met his determined gaze, then nodded. 'All right. I don't need to be checked over, but if it's your price for letting Chris off the hook, I'll pay it.'

'Get in the car,' Richard said. He looked at her cousin. 'Can you manage? What about Sara's bike?'

'I'll get a mate of mine to come and fetch it on his truck.' Chris glanced at Sara apologetically. 'I'll ring you. OK?'

'Yes,' she said. 'Sorry, Chris.'

'Not your fault.'

He stood watching as Richard joined Sara in the car. She waved to him, then stared straight ahead as Richard started the engine. Her expression was one of controlled anger. Obviously, she resented his interference. Well, she could just get on with it. He could be as stubborn as she any day.

'It's for your own good, you know.'

'I'm not a child, Richard. If I were hurt, I would do something about it. It was just a shock that's all.'

'You've been acting like a schoolgirl rather than an experienced nurse. You fainted. You've had a nasty shock. I would prefer it if you have a check-up, just to be sure there's nothing wrong.'

'OK. Fine. I've agreed. End of story.' Her face was set, her expression furious.

Richard held his tongue. He wondered why she was so prickly. She must know that her accident could cause problems which were not immediately noticeable, and that a check-over was routine.

He drove her to the A and E unit at St Saviour's, but when he attempted to follow her inside she stopped him with a fierce look.

'I don't need you to come with me, thank you. I said I'll get myself checked over and I will. I shan't bolt the moment your back is turned. When I make a deal I don't welch on it, OK?'

'I didn't suppose you would.' Richard frowned. 'What's wrong with you? You act as if I was about to kill your pet dog. Just why are you so angry, Sara?'

She turned and looked at him. He saw that her eyes were suspiciously bright, as though she was having difficulty in holding back her tears. That wasn't surprising. For goodness' sake, she'd had a nasty accident. Most women would have wept on his shoulder, but she seemed determined to keep him at a distance.

'Just stay away from me, Richard,' she warned. 'I'm bad news. You don't want to get involved.'

He backed away from her, his hands up, the palms towards her.

'OK. Suit yourself. I was trying to help. Do whatever you want.'

Richard turned and walked away. If she didn't want to know, that was fine with him. Why should he care? He was about to get into his car when some instinct made him glance back. Sara was lying on the ground! He raced back to her. Her eyes were closed and she'd obviously fainted again.

'You silly little idiot,' Richard muttered, his feelings torn between exasperation and concern. 'Just what did you think you were up to?'

He bent down, gathering her up in his arms and carrying her into the brightly lit A and E department. A nurse came hurrying up to him immediately.

'What happened to Sara?' she asked. 'Was it an accident? I've told her she'll kill herself on that stupid bike one of these days.'

'She slid across the road and ended up in a dike,' Richard said. 'I don't think she's badly hurt, but she may have hit her head, though she says not. This is the second time she's fainted since it happened, and I was a bit worried about her.'

'She has seemed a bit off colour this last week or so,' the nurse said, leading Richard towards a cubicle. 'I think she's been eating too little just recently. It's not that she's anorexic—this girl can eat when she wants—believe me—but she's been upset over something.'

Richard laid Sara down carefully on the narrow bed. She was beginning to stir. Her eyelids fluttered and then she opened her eyes. She groaned as she saw Richard.

'You again! I thought you were going?'

'You fainted,' the nurse told her. 'Dr Dalton brought you in.'

'Go away, Maureen,' Sara muttered. 'And take him with you.'

'I'm sorry,' Maureen said, offering her hand to Richard. 'I'm Maureen Young—and this ungrateful wretch shares a house with me and another nurse called Phyllis. She can be normal sometimes, quite human, but this obviously isn't one of those times.'

Richard laughed. Maureen was a very attractive woman, perhaps twenty-six or so, blonde and curvaceous.

'It's nice to meet you,' he said, taking her hand. 'How did you know who I was?'

'I saw you with Jack one evening last month, before you started working here,' Maureen replied. 'It was just before Christmas. You'd been to the pub in the village. You wouldn't have seen me. I was in a car with a friend.'

'I'm glad Sara has someone to look after her.' He grinned at Maureen, liking her friendly manner. 'Will you keep an eye on her for me, please? Make sure she gets a thorough check-over. I don't like that fainting. If she's not eating enough, try and persuade her she would look even more attractive if she put on six or seven pounds.'

'Will do,' Maureen said and smiled. 'It's about time someone started to look out for her, and she doesn't always bother to eat when she's busy. Though I think she's just naturally slim—lucky devil!'

'Hey, you two!' Sara said indignantly. 'Who gave either of you permission to run my life? Stop talking about me as if I were an idiot and go save the world.'

'We might even do that,' Richard retorted but without anger. 'It would help if we didn't have to worry about silly girls who half starve themselves and then fall off their bikes.'

'It was nothing to do with my not eating enough!' Sara glared at him. 'Maybe I did skip lunch today—but I came off because Chris swerved to avoid a dog. Anyone could have done that.'

'That's your excuse. If you ate properly your reactions might improve,' Richard said. 'It might even make you better tempered—but that's asking a lot...'

Sara looked for something to throw.

'Go away, Richard. I hate you. I'm not starving, and I can manage to look after myself. I don't need a nanny, thank you! Your trouble is, you worry too much!'

'You don't know me,' he replied. 'But I have a feeling you're going to...whether you like it or not.'

He blew her a kiss, winked at Maureen and left before Sara could think of a satisfactory answer.

'What was all that about?' Maureen asked after he'd gone. 'Have you gone mad or something? That is one delicious man! If he worried about me I'd swoon, not tell him to get lost.'

Sara made a rude face at her. She knew Maureen was talking sense, but that nagging fear inside her just wouldn't let go—and she couldn't confide in her friend. At least, there was one friend she might be able to talk to, but she wasn't here.

Sara knew she ought to take a few days off after the accident. Just to make sure there was nothing wrong. Perhaps if she could square it with Admin, she would go down to London and stay with Julia.

'So, what are you going to do about it?' Julia asked as they sat cross-legged on the carpet drinking wine spritzers and eating a rather gooey and delicious pizza. 'From what you've told me, you rather fancy Richard Dalton— and if he looks even half as good as you've described, he's very fanciable.'

'You know why all my relationships go wrong,' Sara said. 'I think I like someone enough to...but then at the last moment I draw back. That soon kills any relationship.' She pulled a wry face. 'Besides, he did ask me for coffee and I turned him down—and after the way I went on at him the other night, he's never going to ask me out again.'

'What's wrong with asking him?'

Julia flicked back her long dark hair. She was a vivid girl—startlingly blue eyes, raven black hair, a mouth that was delicately pencilled and coloured with a bright crimson, and a perfect cream complexion. That evening she was wearing black cropped pants and a loose scarlet shirt.

'I only wish I had your confidence,' Sara said, and smiled at her with affection. 'I suppose I do like Richard rather a lot—but that makes it even worse. Supposing I ask him out and then…'

'Most men aren't like Peter Myers,' Julia said, her eyes glinting with anger. 'I wish I could get my hands on him. There wouldn't be enough of him left to pester you, love.'

'I don't suppose he really means to upset me,' Sara admitted. 'What he did to my mother was unspeakable—but it shouldn't make me dislike all men, should it?' She hesitated, knowing she would probably feel much better if she told Julia about the attempt at date rape, but she still couldn't bring herself to share the unpleasant memory—even with her best friend.

'No, of course not. I've told you before, they aren't all like him,' Julia said. She looked at her friend anxiously. 'Don't let that brute ruin your life, too, Sara. I know it hurts that your mother died that way. Nothing is ever going to change that or the fact that Peter let her down—but if you really like Richard, why not give him a chance? He doesn't sound the sort to take advantage. In fact, he sounds a bit like a knight of old—always coming to the rescue.'

'A knight in shining armour?' Sara smiled.

'More like a knight in a white coat,' Julia said. 'If I were you, I'd hold on tight, love. Grab your chance while you can. A man like that isn't going to go begging for long.'

'No…though I think he's had an unhappy experience,' Sara said. 'There was a girl…she died of an overdose, I think… He told me about her but I don't know all the details.'

'That's odd,' Julia said, frowning. 'Did he tell you why she took the drugs?'

'No, except that she had no confidence in herself.'

'Maybe he isn't all that white,' Julia said. 'I know I told you to grab him while you had the chance—but just be careful. You don't want to get hurt again.'

Sara nodded. Julia was thinking of her, but somehow she knew that Richard hadn't been to blame for the girl's death. She also knew that he blamed himself…

Richard didn't see Sara for a few days, even though he visited one of Jack's patients who had been transferred to St Saviour's after having a non-malignant lump removed from his neck. The man was in his seventies and needed extra hospitalization because he lived alone. After spending some ten minutes talking to him, Richard made his way to the staff canteen. He hung around for a while, hoping to see Sara or her friend Maureen.

Sara wasn't there but Maureen came in with three other girls. When she saw him, she left her friends and came over.

'Can I buy you a coffee?' Richard asked. 'Will your friends mind if you sit here for a while?'

'They'll be green with envy,' Maureen said, and laughed. 'But what do I care? If you're worried about Sara, she had a few bruises but nothing more serious. She took a few days off work and went to stay with a friend in London—a nurse called Julia Rossiter.'

Richard nodded. 'Good. I was worried when she fainted twice in succession.'

'She hadn't eaten for hours. She does that sometimes. I think she just forgets, especially if she's upset about something—and she has been for a while now. I don't know why. Sara is a very private person, she doesn't tell anyone much.'

Richard grimaced. 'I don't think Sara likes me much.'

'She may forget to eat sometimes,' Maureen quipped, her eyes bright with mischief, 'but she isn't blind or mad. She likes you—she just doesn't want you to know it.'

'I'll bear that in mind,' Richard said, smiling. 'Thanks for talking to me.'

'My friends are waiting…' Maureen hesitated, then took a pen from her bag and wrote something on a scrap of paper. 'That's Sara's phone number in London. She'll be staying there until Monday.' She pushed it towards him, then stood up. 'You can buy me that coffee if you like.'

Richard nodded. He went up to the counter, bought coffee for Maureen and her friends and carried it to them on a tray, then left. He was thoughtful as he drove back to Jonathan's cottage.

Why was he interested in Sara Linden? She obviously had friends who cared about her. It wasn't as if she needed someone to look out for her—and she'd made it clear she didn't want him around. So why couldn't he get her out of his thoughts?

Richard had never had any trouble in getting a girl to go out with him before. They usually fell over themselves to grab his attention—he had difficulty in fighting them off. That had been a part of Beth's problem. She had been so conscious of the scars, even though he'd sworn they meant nothing to him. He hadn't even noticed them after a while.

They were so tiny. Just a small one at the corner of her left eye, and another, deeper one, under her chin. She had wanted him to operate on her again, pleading with him to make her beautiful.

'But you *are* beautiful,' Richard had told her. 'I couldn't do much to help you, Beth. The worst scars were dealt with after your accident. You can't even see them, but these tiny ones aren't worth the pain. It wouldn't change things. Your life wouldn't be any different.'

God! How he wished he'd never spoken those words! How could he have been so cruel, so thoughtless? He'd known how unsure Beth had been since the accident that had torn her lovely face and left her unable to continue her career.

If Beth had been anything but a photographic model for a famous cosmetics firm, it might have been different. The car crash that had nearly taken her life had certainly ruined her work prospects. Richard had repaired the damage so skilfully that most people would never have known she'd been severely injured, but the camera had picked the scars out with a cruel precision. Her employers had wanted to dump her and had used an escape clause to cancel her contract.

Beth had lost almost everything. Her confidence had been destroyed, her life seemingly empty. Even when Richard had declared himself in love with her and asked her to marry him, it hadn't appeared to restore her faith in herself. She'd suffered from bouts of depression—and in one of those black moods had gone out to buy a bottle of painkillers and tried to take her own life.

Only it hadn't been the simple, easy death she'd imagined. Instead of drifting into a peaceful sleep the way it happened in the movies, Beth had lingered for some weeks in pain and distress.

Richard had watched her die. Beth's pain and tears had torn him apart. She'd told him just why she'd taken those damned pills, and he knew it had been his fault. Before she'd died, Beth had forgiven him, but he wasn't sure he would ever be able to forgive himself.

Because she'd been right. He had loved her, but he hadn't been in love with her. And it was that she hadn't been able to bear.

Richard could still hear her voice accusing him of feeling sorry for her, of asking her to marry him because he thought she needed someone to look after her.

As he locked his car and went into the cottage, Richard tried unsuccessfully to block out the memory. He felt so damned guilty. Somehow he ought to have prevented Beth's death.

So, having been burned once, what was he doing worrying about another girl who'd confessed to being trouble? It would be stupid to get involved, Richard decided. Sara's problems weren't of his making. He wasn't responsible for her—nor did she want him to be. She definitely wasn't a clinging vine, she was a prickly pear!

Taking out the scrap of paper Maureen had given him, he screwed it into a ball and threw it into the fire. It would be madness to become emotionally involved with a girl who obviously didn't want him around!

CHAPTER FOUR

'DO YOU think you could help out on A and E this evening?' Sara had answered her phone to hear the voice of the hospital administrator. 'I know it's a lot to ask but they have so many people down with flu and your wards are pretty quiet at the moment. It's just for one night, until we can arrange for some relief staff. We're having to pull out all the stops tonight, Sister.'

'Yes, of course,' Sara replied. 'I'll come in an hour early and check my G wards, then leave my staff nurse in charge.'

'Thank you. I really appreciate this. I've been at my wit's end to find enough cover for the unit. I've got a couple of juniors, but I need a senior nurse. Where I'm going to find a doctor who will stand in at this late hour I have no idea...'

Sara murmured something sympathetic, then replaced the receiver. A and E wasn't her favourite duty, but the staff there were so overworked that it wasn't surprising they went down like ninepins when a flu epidemic struck.

She'd agreed to go in an hour early, but she was actually there an hour and a half before her normal time. She talked to Sister Martin about the day's influx of patients, made her own check on cases she was already familiar with and waited until Gillian arrived for her shift.

Having made sure that she wouldn't be unduly missed that evening, she went down to A and E to be briefed on what was going on so far.

The unit was quiet when she went in. She saw Richard

60

Dalton almost at once. He was attending to an emergency admission. A mechanic had chopped his finger off while attempting to hoist a heavy engine out of a car. The end of his finger had been sliced through by sharp metal, but the wound had been wrapped and the fingertip had been retrieved.

Sara heard the conversation as the injured man was brought in.

'I wrapped Jim's finger in a sterile lint dressing, Doctor, and also the piece that came off. Then I put that in a bag of ice from the freezer. I hope I did right?'

'That was very quick thinking,' Richard said approvingly. 'It may help us, but we have to do an X-ray to see whether any bone has been lost. It may be possible just to do a skin graft if the bone is intact. Had the finger been severed at the base, we would have needed to reattach it by microsurgery—which would have meant transferring Jim elsewhere. But as it is I think we may be able to do something for him here.'

Sara watched as they all disappeared into one of the curtained cubicles, then turned her attention to the arrival of a young boy who had a foreign body in his eye.

Sara took him into a cubicle and went through the procedure known as triage, where patients were seen almost immediately by a nurse to be assessed as one of three categories—major problems needing immediate attention, major problems needing to be seen as soon as possible, and minor problems.

In this case, the foreign body seemed to be merely a tiny piece of grit, which she was able to locate and remove herself. After making a routine examination of the pupils with her torch, Sara thought the patient's sight was unaffected. However, she asked the boy's mother to wait with him until the doctor came to examine the eye for any damage, then went back out to Reception.

'I've been here since mid-afternoon. It's been mad here,' a voice said behind her, and she swung round to see Richard standing there. He gave her a friendly smile. 'I suppose you've been drafted in to cover for the flu brigade, like me?'

'Yes.' Sara looked at him uncertainly. He would have been justified if he'd shown some resentment after her behaviour the last time they'd met. 'It really has hit us hard this year.'

'And are you feeling better yourself?'

'Yes, I'm fine. Thank you for asking. There was really no need to worry when I came off the bike that evening. I escaped with a few bruises.'

'It wasn't just the fall—'

Richard would have pursued the conversation, but the doors of A and E burst open and a crowd of noisy young men trooped in. Two of them had blood pouring from their noses, and it was obvious that they'd been fighting.

'Here we go,' Sara said, and went off to start sorting the group out.

Richard joined her immediately.

'Right,' he said. 'Let's keep the noise down a bit, please. If you have an injury report to Reception. Names and addresses, please, then sit down and wait. You will all be seen as soon as possible. Anyone who is just here with a friend, sit down now so we can sort you out.'

The tone of authority in his voice helped to quieten them a bit, but Sara had noted that one or two were the worse for drink. She took one of the young men who was bleeding profusely into a cubicle to make her first assessment. As she was bending over him to wipe away the blood with a sterile swab, the youth made a grab at her thigh.

'Please, don't do that,' she said, frowning at him.

'Why not?' he asked in a slurred voice. 'You've got a lovely bum, Nurse.'

Sara gave him a quelling stare, then went back out to Reception. Richard was still in the thick of it, sorting out the more rowdy of the youths.

'Mr Rowe has a cut on his forehead that looks as if it will need stitching, Doctor. It's not urgent, but it is quite deep.'

'I'll have a look at him.' Richard frowned. 'What's wrong—did he upset you?'

'He made a pass,' Sara replied, shrugging. 'It's par for the course on A and E. Most of them do if they've been drinking. Don't worry, he wasn't violent. I can handle his sort.'

Richard looked grim but didn't say anything. It was one of the hazards of being on night duty in A and E— and it had got worse since his junior houseman days. He knew it must be a constant problem for the nurses—particularly those who looked like Sara Linden.

However, when he examined Mr Rowe, he realized that Sara had been right. The youth might have made a pass, but he wasn't violent, nor was he in a condition to do much more than make silly remarks.

'How did this happen?' Richard asked as he pulled on rubber gloves and swabbed the deep cut. 'It looks as if you've been hit by a bottle, but you've been lucky— there's no sign of splinters.'

'We had an argument. Nothing much…'

Richard nodded. One of the junior nurses had brought in a sterile trolley. He smiled at her and told her he could manage. Judging by the way things were going, she might be needed elsewhere.

It was a simple procedure to clean and then close the wound. He worked neatly and efficiently, the skill he'd neglected this past year flowing back into his fingers. It was a good feeling, something he'd missed.

'There,' he said after a few minutes. 'You'll live. You will probably have a splitting headache, but the painkillers will help.'

'Can I go now?'

'Not for a while. You'll need someone to take you home. Can we phone someone for you—your parents?'

'Nah.' The youth pulled a face. 'Me mates will look after me.'

'Not those who've been drinking,' Richard said. 'Or you'll be back here in a worse state. Get yourselves a taxi—but stay here for twenty minutes or so just in case.'

Richard went into the next cubicle. Sara had cleaned up a bloody nose. The wound was superficial and needed no surgical treatment. Richard did a few routine checks to make sure the youth hadn't suffered concussion, then nodded to Sara.

'He can go with his friend when he's ready.'

The unit was beginning to fill up. A woman had been brought in with what looked like a broken wrist, and a nurse reported the arrival of a man with severe pain in his lower left side.

'He's staying with his daughter at the moment and has been seeing a consultant at his local hospital,' she explained. 'I've sent a fax for his notes—but his daughter says he was being assessed for an operation for a thinning of the aorta…'

Richard frowned. 'In that case he may need emergency surgery. It's too complicated a procedure for the theatre staff we have here. You should telephone the nearest hospitals capable of doing the operation and see who can take him. Tell them we may be sending an emergency through. Brief them on the situation and ask them to have their consultant on standby.'

'Yes, sir. Will you examine Mr Smith now or when his notes come through?'

'The notes could take too long,' Richard said. 'I'll take a look at him now and then I shall want to speak to his daughter.'

He went into the cubicle she indicated. The patient was a man in his fifties, and he was clearly in great pain. As the aorta was the main trunk of the arterial system of the body, if there was a slight rupture, speed was of the essence.

'You've been having the pain for a while?' Richard said, checking the patient's vital signs. His blood pressure was beginning to drop. Time was now all-important.

'Yes, but not like this. I've never felt anything like this before.'

'Your condition has obviously worsened suddenly. Were you intending to have an operation, Mr Smith?'

'I had just begun having the tests,' he replied. 'My doctor sent me to Addenbrookes, which is near my home town, and they thought it was a thinning of a valve. But they weren't sure whether to operate or not because of my chest. I have a bit of bronchitis, you see.'

'Yes, I see.' Richard took his blood pressure and frowned. It wasn't good. 'I think you need to have surgery immediately, Mr Smith. I don't think we have a choice any more.'

'What are my chances?'

'Reasonably good,' Richard said. 'Had we not been aware of your problem it might have caused a fatal delay, but as it is I'm going to have you transferred to a suitable hospital straight away. King's Lynn is the nearest if they can take you. A surgical team will be waiting for you in Theatre. I'm going to give you something for the pain now. You'll become drowsy and you won't know much of what's going on until you wake up, when you'll be in Intensive Care.' He smiled at the patient. 'I'll send your daughter in to you now.'

Richard left the cubicle. Mr Smith's daughter came up to him immediately, looking anxious.

'Is my father going to be all right?'

'We have to operate,' Richard told her. 'It is no longer a case of whether we ought to—if we don't he'll certainly die. I think he may have ruptured or be on the point of it, which means we have to act quickly.'

'But will he survive an operation? His own doctor was worried about his chest.' She gulped back her tears. 'I feel so guilty, Doctor. I work, you see, and I don't get much time to visit him. I hadn't realized he was this ill until last Sunday and now this...'

'We all have our own lives to lead. You mustn't blame yourself too much. The love you have for him is obvious.'

'Yes, of course. I just hope he's going to pull through.'

'I can't pretend it is going to be straightforward,' Richard said, deciding to be brutally frank. 'But he has a reasonable chance. What we're actually going to do is insert a little V-shaped plastic tube into the abdominal...' He saw her frightened face and touched her hand. 'I can't guarantee he will come through, but in my own experience I would say that we have a good chance of success, simply because his own doctor spotted the problem and alerted his consultant.'

'Then if he does survive it will be due to his own doctor,' she said, her eyes bright with tears.

'And the skill of the surgeons,' Richard said. 'But certainly, if this had not been investigated prior to this evening it would have made your father's chances of survival far less likely.'

She nodded. 'Thank you. May I see him now? I think he must be very frightened.'

She went into the cubicle, and Richard heard her voice, strong and positive. 'You're going to be all right, Dad. The doctor says they've caught it in time. You'll have lots of wires and things sticking out of you when you wake up, I expect, but he says you'll come through with flying colours.'

She had the right attitude, Richard thought. He could only hope that her words proved prophetic.

The ambulance crew had arrived to take Mr Smith to a hospital that had agreed to accommodate him. They told Richard that they'd arranged to take him to a landing pad where he would be transferred to a helicopter. In a case like this there was no time to waste. Richard saw him on his way, then got back to work.

The tempo picked up as the evening progressed, with cases ranging from a young girl who had overdosed on crack to a child with head injuries, besides several more youths, all of whom had been drinking and fighting.

Richard hardly had a chance to speak to Sara, but he was able to observe her with the patients. He was pleased to discover she was more than capable, her manner a little reserved towards the men perhaps, except with elderly patients, for whom she seemed to have a special affinity.

It was towards the early hours of the morning when two of the youths that had been treated earlier came back to the department. One of them had been vomiting, and his friend was shouting abuse at the nurses.

'He's ill,' he said, using foul language as one of the nurses tried to tell him to sit down. 'You bastards stuck a plaster on him and sent him home. You're too damned full of your own sh—'

'Please, sit down, sir,' Sara said, taking hold of his arm. 'If your friend is ill he'll be—'

The drunk hit out at her, sending her reeling back. She gave a cry of pain, and Richard saw her mouth had been cut by a ring on the drunk's hand.

'Leave this to me,' he said as he passed her. 'Get back out of the way, Sara.'

He approached the two youths, realizing it was the one with the bloodied nose he'd treated earlier who was vomiting.

'Calm down,' he said to the youth's friend. 'And don't touch my nurses again. If you attempt to hit any member of my staff I shall send for the police.'

'You're the bastard who sent him home…'

'Help me get him into a cubicle and I'll take another look,' Richard said. 'And don't give me any more of your foul mouth or I'll see you spend the rest of the night in a cell, and I promise you'll feel sorry for yourself.'

The youth glared at him, but Richard was bigger and obviously strong, and the warning look in his eyes left little to the imagination.

'I'm worried about me mate. What's wrong with him?'

'We'll take a look, shall we?' He turned to the second youth. 'So, what seems to be the problem, Mr Sallis? Does your head hurt?' He held a pencil up in front of his eyes. 'Follow this…left…now right.' Then he shone a torch in the patient's eyes, his gaze narrowing in sudden suspicion. 'You're sweating... Tell me, have you got pain in your stomach?'

'Yeah...and I feel sick...' He suited his actions to his words, vomiting onto the floor beside the bed. 'And I'm hot...'

'How long have you felt this way?'

'A few hours...'

'Before you started fighting?'

'Yeah...most of the day...'

Richard nodded, and looked at the youth who had hit Sara. 'Your friend has the flu. There's nothing we can do for him here. Get yourselves a taxi and go home, both of you. Your friend should be in bed. Tell him to drink plenty of fluids and keep warm.'

The youth looked at his mate in disgust, then hauled him off the bed, dragging him out of the cubicle. He was swearing as they left the department together.

Richard went in search of Sara. She was sitting in the staff restroom, holding a pad of gauze to her lip.

'Let me have a look at that,' he said, and went to crouch down in front of her. 'I'm sorry he hit you, Sara.'

'It was my own fault for going near him,' she said. 'I could see what sort of state he was in. I should have known better. We usually have a couple of male nurses on at night to handle the rowdy cases, but most of. them are down with the flu.'

Richard said nothing. He looked at the cut on her mouth. It had stopped bleeding, but would obviously be sore.

'It doesn't need stitching,' he said. 'Do you want a dressing or just leave it open?'

'I'm not walking around with a dressing stuck over my mouth,' Sara said, and winced. 'Ouch! It hurts to talk.'

'Then don't,' Richard advised. 'Look, we're almost

finished here. The next shift will be on in ten minutes. Why don't you go home?'

'Would you mind?' Sara gazed into his eyes. 'I feel as if I'll fall down soon anyway.'

'You go, then.' He smiled at her. 'Me...I could do another shift. I don't need much sleep.'

She nodded. 'I think I owe you an apology, Richard. You helped me the night I came off the bike and I was rude to you...'

'Not rude,' he said. 'Just a bit prickly. I got the idea I wasn't your favourite person.'

Sara chuckled, then winced. 'Don't make me laugh. It hurts. Maureen read me the Riot Act. I think I ought to make amends in some way.'

'It doesn't matter,' Richard replied. 'Forget it, Sara.'

She looked at him uncertainly. 'It's Maureen's birthday next weekend. We've hired a hall and we're having a disco. I don't suppose you would want to come?'

'Are you asking?' Richard's brows went up as she nodded. 'Then I'm accepting. I would like to come, Sara. I should like it if we could be friends. I haven't been living here long. It would be good to make some friends locally.'

She looked at him oddly. 'You really meant it when you asked if we could be friends, didn't you?'

'Yes—why not?'

She shrugged. 'I don't know...except most men I meet want to jump in bed with me five minutes after they've bought me a drink, and if I say no they get nasty...'

'Oh, I usually wait at least half an hour,' Richard said, smiling at her. 'You should give that sort the elbow, Sara. I promise I'll give you plenty of warning if I'm going to come on to you—and I won't get angry if you say no.'

'Promise?' Her eyes met his. 'I'd like to be friends,

Richard. I do like you, and I'm sick of fighting off all the crawlers!'

Richard solemnly saluted her. 'Friends, Scout's honour.'

'Ouch!' Sara put her hand to her mouth. 'Stop making me laugh.'

'Go home and put some ice on that,' Richard advised, 'then get some sleep.'

'Yes, I will,' she said. 'And thanks, Richard.'

'For what?' he asked, raising his brows.

'For just being you...'

Sara sighed as she put out the light, then slid into bed. She was so tired. She just hoped she wasn't going down with flu herself. It would be a shame to miss Maureen's party, now that she'd finally got around to asking Richard.

She smiled sleepily to herself as she reviewed the night's events. Richard had come to her rescue once again, and it had felt good. He really was a nice person— no, nice didn't fit Richard Dalton at all! He was too attractive, too...dynamic to be dismissed as merely nice.

Sara knew that he affected her in a way no other man ever had. She enjoyed being near him, and the touch of his hand didn't send shivers of revulsion through her, which had been the case too often in the past.

Was it possible she was falling in love with him?

She smiled to herself, pleased that she'd taken Julia's advice. She wouldn't have dared if he hadn't turned up at A and E so unexpectedly.

'Maybe it is fate,' she murmured, then fell asleep wondering where Richard was now, and what he was thinking about her.

*   *   *

Richard had decided it was time he got round to returning the Range Rover to its rightful owner and buying himself a new car. And he'd seen something he rather liked earlier in the week. He would pop into the garage and sign the necessary papers that afternoon.

He was thoughtful as he slid behind the wheel. He seemed to have reached a landmark in his life. For a long time he'd believed it was impossible to put the past behind him and move on. Now he suddenly felt the shadows beginning to lift.

He would always retain some guilt, of course. Richard couldn't deny his part in Beth's tragic death. He would never do that, but he was starting to see that it might be possible to live with his memories. He might even be able to return to the work he loved without an intolerable burden of guilt.

Beth had hated it when he'd had to cancel a social engagement because a patient had needed him. After her death, it had been impossible for him to simply carry on as if nothing had happened, but he was beginning to realize he needed the fulfillment his real work had always given him.

Surgeons were born, not made. One of his tutors had told him that and he believed it was true. He'd started out with the intention of being a GP, but something had driven him on. He knew now that he would never be at peace with himself until he returned to his vocation.

What had brought about the change? Richard wasn't sure. Being with his family over Christmas had undoubtedly helped, but he had the oddest notion that the healing process had really begun on New Year's Eve, when he'd stepped in to rescue Sara from the bully who'd been hurting her.

Could it be that he'd begun to feel something for Sara?

Something more than the concern he would have felt for any young woman who'd seemed vulnerable? Except that she wasn't, not really.

She'd been unhappy the night he'd first seen her, but she would probably have handled the situation without his help. She was a rather determined young woman, well able to stand up for herself most of the time. She hadn't made a fuss, even when that drunken lout had attacked her in A and E.

Richard sensed Sara's feelings had been badly hurt at some time, and because of it she'd fallen into the habit of keeping all men at arm's length. He wasn't sure just why that independent young woman had got under his skin, but she had.

He realized that he was looking forward to the disco that weekend. Working with her at A and E was one thing, but actually being with her at a party was something else.

Perhaps he could begin to get to know her. It wouldn't be easy. Sara had drawn the lines quite firmly. Well, that was all right. The last thing Richard wanted at this moment of his life was a cheap sexual fling. He needed to put down roots, to make friends, and feel a part of something after his months in the wilderness.

It might be that he and Sara would never be more than friends, but women who were easy conquests had always bored him. Getting past the barrier Sara had erected was a challenge, and might even be fun. It would certainly be interesting.

CHAPTER FIVE

SARA wasn't asked to stand in on A and E again that week, and for once her own wards seemed to be running at a manageable level. Her tour of night duty was almost over, and she would be transferring to days after the weekend, which was a free period.

She'd had some qualms about seeing Richard at Maureen's party, but tried not to panic. He'd offered friendship, for goodness' sake! Just because she'd invited him to a disco, that didn't mean he would think she was inviting him to sleep with her…and yet she couldn't help thinking it might be rather nice to be kissed by Richard Dalton. He had a very kissable mouth.

Just thinking about his mouth was disturbing. She felt an odd flutter deep down inside her, a feeling that was becoming familiar whenever she saw him. Maureen was right, he was a gorgeous man!

Sara had thought she might see him around the village when she did her shopping, but she didn't see any sign of him. Angela and Jack Harper had returned from their brief holiday, and Sara discovered why Richard wasn't about when she popped in to see his sister on the Friday morning.

'I haven't seen you for ages,' Angela said. 'Not since Christmas. What have you been doing with yourself?'

'Oh, this and that,' Sara replied. 'We've been very busy at St Saviour's, and I was away for a couple of days—and then you were.' Her true reason was rather different, but Sara kept it to herself.

'Yes, I know. I finally managed to drag Jack away from his patients,' Angela said with a wry grin. 'Only because my brother has been standing in for him. It's a miracle we managed to get Richard here, you know. It isn't his sort of work, not really. He's a brilliant plastic surgeon—or he was until about eighteen months ago…' She frowned. 'Something happened in New York. I'm not sure what—I think it may have been a woman. He suddenly gave up his job and went off to Africa…'

'Yes…' Sara looked at her thoughtfully. She'd heard whispers about Richard having been in plastic surgery— and the reasons for him apparently having given it up. 'He did mention he'd been abroad. We met…at Jonathan Thirstone's New Year party.'

'Oh, did you go to that?' Angela asked, looking at her curiously. 'You met my brother there? Richard and Jon go back a long way, of course—that's where Richard is at the moment, actually. Jonathan wants him to take on some specialized surgery at his clinic. Richard resisted at first, made all sorts of excuses, but now I think he's con-sidering it. Jack and his partners believe they've found someone suitable to join the practice so Richard won't be needed here for much longer. It was always going to be a temporary measure.'

Sara's heart plummeted. She'd begun to think that per-haps Richard might be serious about their relationship, but if he was going away it would be just another casual affair. If she let it go that far!

'Something wrong?' Angela asked, looking at her oddly as a sigh escaped her.

'No, nothing at all,' Sara lied. 'I'm just a little tired, I suppose.'

'Yes, you do look tired. Perhaps you need a holiday.'

'Perhaps,' Sara said, and then pulled a face. 'To be

honest, I don't really know what I want. Maybe an entirely new me.'

'We'd all like that,' Angela said, and grinned. 'I should like to be size ten, very rich, very beautiful and famous— how's that for starters?'

'I think I'd settle for the very rich,' Sara said, and began to giggle. 'You've just made me feel very much better.'

Sara took a few minutes to call in on Mr Ross. She'd bought a few grapes at the local supermarket and she gave them to his wife as she was invited into the neat cottage.

'He will be so pleased to see you,' Mrs Ross told her, leading the way through the hall. 'I've heard nothing but how wonderful Sister Linden was to him in the hospital—and it's good of you to visit us like this. You must be so busy.'

'I've got a few hours off,' Sara said. 'We all loved your husband on the ward, Mrs Ross. He's a real charmer.'

'Ah, he is that,' the old lady twinkled at her. 'You should have seen him after he was demobbed, Sister. He was more handsome than Clark Gable, and all the girls were after him! Still, we don't tell the men that sort of thing, do we? It isn't good for them.'

Sara laughed. She knew that Mrs Ross herself suffered from a heart problem, and the couple must be finding it very difficult to cope, but they were very cheerful. It was an example to others who didn't have half their problems, and it made Sara realize how lucky she was. She was glad she'd taken the time to call. Sometimes when a patient went home you lost all contact, but living in a small community like this it made it easier to stay in touch.

'That nice Dr Dalton was here again yesterday,' Mrs Ross said. 'He says everything's going along nicely so we can't grumble, can we?'

'I think we all grumble too much these days,' Sara said. 'I know I do—and I shouldn't.'

'Well, I'll put the kettle on,' Mrs Ross said. 'You go and sit with my husband and have a nice chat, dear. I should think you can do with a sit-down all the chasing around you do.'

Richard had made arrangements to check out the clinic on that Friday morning. Jonathan was unable to be there himself, but had been enthusiastic on the phone.

'Does this mean you're considering joining us?'

'It means I want to see the facilities you have, Jon, that's all.'

'I'm sure the consortium would consider buying any new technology you felt necessary. As I told you, we've been offering routine surgery, but with you on board…it would open up all sorts of possibilities, Rich. We could attract an international clientele…'

'Don't get too excited,' Richard warned. 'I'm only thinking about the possibility of a return to surgery. I might not even be up to my former standard after a break of several months. My kind of surgery is very demanding, as you know. I might have lost my edge.'

'Don't be an idiot,' Jonathan said. 'Of course you haven't. It's something you never forget—like riding a bike. I wish I could be there to show you round, but I'll let them know you're on your way.'

'Thanks. I'll be there about lunchtime.'

'We've got a good chef. It will give you a chance to try him out.'

Richard laughed. 'You won't bribe me that way, Jon.

But if I like what I see I may consider joining you—perhaps on a part-time basis.'

'Whatever. I know my partners would be glad to have you on your own terms. You may think we don't know what you did in New York but, let me assure you, your reputation has gone before you.'

'Don't flatter me too much. I haven't said yes yet.'

Richard was smiling as he replaced the receiver. He could make the trip, which was really only a short distance in a decent car, and return in time to be ready for work that evening. He wanted to have a lie-in on Saturday so that he was fresh for the party Sara had invited him to, but that wouldn't present a problem.

He thought he might even find time to buy a gift for Maureen on the way over.

In actual fact, Richard found just the gift he wanted for Maureen's birthday in the small boutique at the Rosewell clinic. The drive down had been easy in the two-year-old Mercedes estate car he'd purchased earlier that week. The main roads had been busy for the first part of his journey, but when he turned off onto the winding country lanes that led to the clinic he met very little traffic.

The Rosewell was an old country house, gracious and lovely in the glow of the winter sunshine. It was easy to see why clients who could afford to would pay to come here for treatment, so much nicer than the majority of busy hospitals. The gardens were extensive, and there was a small lake with a picturesque wooden bridge. It was also just a few miles inland from a variety of coastal resorts, the nearest being Blakeny, a very beautiful and still unspoiled area of marshes and salt creeks that led to the sea.

The chief nursing officer, who would have been called Matron a few years previously, met him in Reception.

'Sylvia Bennet,' she told him as they shook hands. 'Dr Thirstone rang me to tell me to expect you. Shall I take you for a tour now, or would you prefer to have lunch first?'

'I have to get back because I'm working this evening,' Richard said. 'A quick tour of the clinic, and perhaps a little more time in Theatre…unless it is being used?'

'There's an operation in progress at the moment,' she replied, 'but I'm sure Mr Rush wouldn't object if you wanted to observe. It is a routine hip replacement and has been under way for some time.'

'We'll see,' Richard said. 'A tour of the rest, please, then we'll see what stage they've reached in Theatre, shall we?'

'Mr Rush will probably be finished in about half an hour, sir.'

Although it was an extremely large building, the clinic itself was only a small part of the whole. Most of the rooms were for patients recovering from treatment carried out elsewhere or just taking a rest from their hectic lives. There were all the usual facilities expected in an exclusive place of this kind—a gym, sauna, massage areas and a swimming pool, besides all the outdoor courts and rinks for tennis and bowls.

The medical staff had their own community rooms and there were offices available for use by visiting consultants. There was also the boutique, where Richard bought some perfume for Maureen, then as an afterthought bought a different brand for Sara.

He had coffee and a salad sandwich in the staff canteen, resisting all Sylvia Bennet's attempts to persuade him into a three-course lunch in the main dining room, then asked if the theatre was free.

It was, and, after donning scrubs and sterile boots, he was allowed to spend time looking around the very modern and well-equipped theatre by himself. He was pleasantly surprised to discover much of the technology he had been accustomed to in America was already available, though there were a couple of gaps he would raise with Jonathan…if he decided to take up his offer.

He still wasn't sure about that as he began the drive back. Yet he'd liked what he'd seen at the Rosewell, and it might fit well with the other ideas that had begun to form in his mind.

He would have to make some enquiries, but for the moment he needed to concentrate on getting back to the cottage. He actually felt tired for the first time in ages, and he could do with a couple of hours' sleep before he was back on call.

Sara was reading the letter when Maureen came in with the shopping. Her first instinct was to hide it, but then she decided it was time she confided in her friend.

'It's a letter from Peter Myers—my stepfather. You remember I told you a bit about him the other night?'

'You told me he was bothering you with phone calls all the time. What has he done now?'

'He wants to come and see me. This is the second letter I've had from him. I didn't answer the first.'

'Why, are you afraid he will start threatening you again?'

'No—not really.' Sara sighed. 'I think he wants to make things right between us, but I can't forgive him for what he did. Mum was so miserable, so sure he'd been cheating on her. She died calling for him but he didn't come.'

'Maybe he was miserable, too. And a bit of a coward. Some people can't watch the people they love suffer. You should know that, Sara. You've seen it before.'

Sara looked at her thoughtfully. Her stepfather had protested his innocence all along, but she'd believed her mother. She still believed her, but for the first time in months she was beginning to feel better about things. Maybe it was telling Maureen, but Sara had a sneaking feeling that some of her sense of release was due to meeting Richard.

All at once, she was looking forward to seeing him that evening.

Sara greeted Richard as soon as he entered the hall where the disco was being held. She smiled at him, and told him she liked the shirt he was wearing. It was black silk and very sexy.

'I bought it from the shop you told me about that day we met in Royston,' Richard said. She was wearing cropped, tight pants and a black top. 'I like your outfit, Sara. It's very trendy, and it suits you.'

'You mean it's not quite as tarty as the dress I was wearing on New Year's Eve.' Sara chuckled as she saw the look in his eyes. 'No, don't try to deny it, Richard. That was a mistake, believe me. I was feeling defiant. I wanted to hit out at the world in general. This is the start of the new me. I'm glad you approve.'

'I do,' he said, 'and not because you looked tarty that night either. I would have said provocative was more the word we're looking for here. Would I be wrong to assume it was a challenge to any man who dared to notice?'

Sara laughed again, a husky, warming sound that was

very attractive. She was in a party mood, and felt as if she were lit up from inside. A number with a fast beat suddenly blared out and she grabbed his hand, pulling him towards the bar.

'Dump the wine,' she insisted, 'and Maureen's present. I love this one. Come and dance with me.'

Maureen was behind the bar. She smiled at Richard as he deposited his parcels and allowed himself to be dragged onto the floor.

Richard wouldn't have called himself a brilliant disco dancer, but he didn't have to be. All he had to do was move in time to the beat and follow Sara's twisting, twirling feet around the floor.

There was no doubt that she was a fantastic dancer, a natural mover. Her body snaked through the intricate steps she performed, her hips swaying in an intoxicating rhythm that any red-blooded male would find fascinating…as several other men in the room surely did if the way their heads turned to watch her was anything to go by. She was a magnet, a live wire, fizzing with energy.

'You're a wonderful dancer,' Richard said when at last the music ended. 'You could do it professionally.'

'I suppose I could,' she said, her eyes bright with laughter as she gazed up at him. 'I took dancing classes when I was small…' For a moment her eyes clouded as the painful memory struck home. *Peter dropping her off outside the classes and telling her to have fun.* 'But that's all in the past. I don't want to dance professionally. I like dancing for fun—and I like being a nurse. I want to help people.'

'Yes, I've already gathered that. You're particularly good with elderly people. I noticed that the other evening.'

'Thank you.' Sara smiled, feeling a little shy. 'That's

another reason why I haven't given Jonathan Thirstone an answer about the job he offered me. I would have to do general nursing at the clinic.'

'But you have considered it? Moving to the Rosewell?'

It seemed to be important to him. Sara wondered why.

Maureen was coming towards them with a couple of drinks. Her arrival prevented Sara from giving him an answer.

'That was a lovely wine you gave us, Richard,' Maureen said. 'I've sneaked you both a glass before it all disappears.' She held out her wrist to Sara, inviting her to smell. 'It's a gorgeous perfume. Richard bought it for me.' She smiled at him. 'You're too generous. I didn't expect anything like this.'

'It's nothing,' he replied. 'I'm glad you like it.'

'I love it,' she replied. 'Don't let Sara monopolize you all evening. I'm not as good as her, but I like to dance.'

She gave him a flirtatious look over her shoulder as she walked away.

Sara was sipping her wine. 'Maureen was right, this is good. Most people buy plonk for these parties, Richard. It must have cost you a fortune.'

'Not that I noticed,' he replied. 'Besides, I like to give my friends presents, and I'm not broke just yet.'

Sara looked at him uncertainly. 'You know the hospital gossips have started on you, don't you?'

'What do they say?' Richard asked wryly. 'Are you wondering how a man who's available for emergency work can afford good wine?'

'Well…' Sara laughed and shook her head. 'To be honest, you've got them stumped, Richard. No one seems to know much about you, other than the fact that you're Dr Harper's brother-in-law—and that you were a surgeon in America. Before you went abroad…'

'Africa,' Richard said, eyes gleaming as he sensed her interest. What the gossips said didn't matter to either of them, it was Sara who wanted to know about his recent past.

He paused. 'What can I tell you? I spent several months walking from village to village with a backpack, and I visited as many medical missions as I could. It was part of a research project that an American friend of mine wanted me to undertake. He was out there himself for a couple of months, but had to return to the States. I was at a loose end so he asked me if I would take over his work, which I did—at least, I observed and took notes for him in between bouts of being angry and feeling sorry for myself.'

'I can't imagine you letting anything get to you that badly.'

'You'd be surprised,' Richard said. 'For a while there, the anger almost managed to destroy me—along with the guilt and remorse, that is.'

'You must have loved her very much…whoever she was.'

'I loved her,' Richard agreed. 'But there was more to it…'

Sara raised her brows, but he shook his head. 'No, not tonight. We're here to have fun, and I have to be on call by midnight.' He put his glass down after one sip. 'I'll stick to water from now on.'

'Me, too,' Sara said. She had finished her wine, and she placed the empty glass beside Richard's full one on a window-ledge. 'One glass is my limit.'

'A very wise decision,' Richard said, and gave her his lazy grin. He held out his hand to her as another fast number began. 'This sounds like our cue to get out there.'

Sara laughed. 'You're beginning to know me,' she said.

'And to like what I know,' Richard replied, and one finger caressed the back of the hand he held.

Sara blushed, but she didn't immediately pull her hand from his and that was a beginning.

Richard danced every fast number with Sara, but on the one occasion she excused herself to go to the bathroom he asked Maureen for the next dance. It was a quarter past eleven when Sara came back to where he was standing, chatting to some of the other doctors and nurses he had met at St Saviour's. He turned to look at her, raising his brows as she hesitated, not saying anything.

'Would you like to dance again?' he asked.

Sara shook her head. 'Not really.' She laughed ruefully. 'I think I've burned up all my energy for one night. I was wondering…would you mind taking me home, Richard?'

'Of course not,' he said at once. 'I should enjoy having a few minutes alone with you before I have to go to work. This has been fun, but you can't talk properly above the noise.'

'No…' Sara smiled. 'I'll get my coat. Two minutes.'

He waited by the door until she came back, smiling at her as she took his arm and looked up at him.

'So…' she said. 'You were telling me about Africa earlier. I caught bits of it, but not all. What were you doing before you went out there?'

'Working in America at a private clinic,' Richard said. 'I was a surgeon, Sara. We specialized in reconstructive work for trauma or cancer patients, but we also did some cosmetic work—it paid the bills.'

Sara smiled. 'Yes, I knew you'd been working in that field. Angela told me the other day. I've known your sister for a few months—but I didn't know she had a brother until you turned up at St Saviour's.'

They were outside the disco, the music still throbbing away, drifting into the night. It was cold and there was a crisp frost on the parked vehicles.

'Angela said you might be leaving here soon…'

'That's possible, yes. I'm not sure yet where I'm going to settle. I may stay in England a couple of years, then go back to America.'

'I see.'

'I've only just started to consider the possibility of going back to surgery,' Richard admitted as he held the door of his car open for her. 'For a while I thought I might make a complete change, but I discovered I need to do it. I might divide my time between the NHS and the Rosewell. It would make for variety, and I rather think I owe something to the country that trained me. So I may stay for longer. I haven't made up my mind.'

Sara nodded, her face hidden from him as she slid into his car.

'This is nice, Richard.' Her hand stroked the leather seats. 'I don't think I've been in a Mercedes before.'

'It's not new,' he replied. 'I need to be working before I can splash out too much, but it's an improvement on what I was driving before.'

'Much nicer,' Sara said. 'I like it—though the Range Rover can be fun off-road. My cousin borrows an old one sometimes to transport his bikes when they're racing at some out-of-the-way place.' She hesitated, then said, 'I was going to ask if you would like to come with us tomorrow. It's just a small meeting. Not one of the season's real events. Just a few friends having a race for fun…'

'I should enjoy that, Sara,' he said, and was rewarded with a smile. 'What time do I pick you up?'

'Can you manage ten o'clock?' she asked, looking at him doubtfully. 'I know you said you don't need much sleep…'

'I hadn't been sleeping at all until I came home,' Richard said. 'But I managed a few hours this morning. I'll be there at ten.'

'Chris will be taking the bikes on his friend's truck,' Sara said. 'I know where to take you—it may be a bit muddy. You'll have to clean your nice new car.'

'I haven't returned the Range Rover yet,' Richard said. 'I was going to do it on Friday but I drove down to the Rosewell and didn't get time. Freddie won't mind if I use it one more day.'

'That's all right, then,' Sara said, looking relieved. 'I was a bit hesitant to ask once I saw the car.'

'Is that all that was bothering you?'

Sara turned to look at him, but he was concentrating on the road ahead and couldn't meet her gaze.

'I'm not sure what you mean.'

'You're not going to back off now you know what I do?' Richard asked. 'I know some of the nurses think surgeons can be pompous idiots who imagine they're some sort of omnipotent beings and have the right to treat the rest of the medical staff like something the cat brought in.'

'In a way they do have to play God sometimes,' Sara said, a lilt of laughter in her voice. 'And one or two of them are a bit like that, though not all of them, of course. Don't worry, Richard. I shan't hold it against you. You don't behave as if you're something special. You're just like the rest of us.'

'Thank you,' Richard said. 'I take that as a compliment.'

'It was meant to be.'

'I'm glad we're friends now, Sara.'

Sara didn't reply to his statement. She felt comfortable and at ease, and there didn't seem any need to reply. The next time she spoke was to tell him where to turn off in the village.

'The house I share with Maureen and Phyllis is just up this road,' Sara said. 'You can come in for a coffee, if you like.'

Richard thought about it. He had twenty minutes before he was due to relieve Jack on call. Not long enough to have the kind of conversation he wanted to have with her.

'If you don't mind, I'll leave that for another day,' he said as he drew the car to a standstill in front of the house she indicated. 'We can sit here for a couple of minutes, if that's all right?'

'Yes,' she said, and turned in her seat to look at him. 'You'll need to put something warm on tomorrow, Richard. It can be very cold, standing around in a muddy field.'

'Thanks for warning me,' he said. 'I'll see what I can borrow from Jack.' He hesitated, then reached into his pocket, taking out the small but distinctive bag containing the perfume he'd bought for her. 'This is for you, Sara. I hope you like it.'

She looked uncertain, then took the perfume out and stared at it. Her gaze lifted to his, her eyes a wonderful bluish haze of colour, but puzzled.

'It's lovely, Richard. But why did you buy it for me? It isn't my birthday.'

'Hasn't anyone ever given you a present just for the

pleasure of giving?' he asked. 'It doesn't have strings attached, Sara. I don't expect you to fall into bed with me. I'm not saying that won't happen one day…but if it does, it will be because we both want it very much. Not because I bought you a present.'

Sara's cheeks were flushed, and she was looking down at the perfume in her lap.

'It's lovely,' she whispered, a croaking sound in her throat. 'I'm sorry if I'm not being very gracious, Richard. No one has ever done anything like this for me before. Chris and my aunt…well, birthdays and Christmas, you know. But nothing like this.'

'It's just a bottle of perfume,' Richard said, feeling a constriction in his throat. Just for a moment she'd let the mask drop and he saw the girl beneath—a girl who was a little frightened but trying very hard not to be. He was very tempted to take her in his arms and kiss her, but he didn't want to spoil things. He'd given her the perfume without an ulterior motive and it had to stay that way. 'You've given me this evening, Sara—and you've invited me to share your fun tomorrow. I think we're quits.'

'OK.' Her head went up, a glitter in her eyes. He knew the barrier was back in place. She wasn't quite ready to trust him yet, at least not enough to let him inside that private place she held deep within herself. 'Don't be late in the morning, Richard—and don't forget to bring some wellington boots if you have them.'

'I can't borrow those from Jack,' he said, and laughed. 'We don't have the same size feet. But I have a pair of walking boots that should be sufficient.'

Sara nodded, then leaned towards him. Her lips just grazed his in the lightest of kisses, then she was opening the door and running up to the front of the house. She had kissed him once before, but this had more feeling.

He sensed that she was beginning to trust him, and that made him feel good.

Richard watched until she was safely inside. He was aware of feeling something he hadn't felt for a very long time. Sara's kiss had aroused a hunger in him.

It was a good thing she'd made her escape before he'd had time to respond to that kiss!

CHAPTER SIX

SARA undressed, then sat in front of her mirror and brushed her hair. Her lips still tingled, she could still taste Richard on them, and it felt good. She realized with a shock that she would have liked to go on kissing him—that she would have liked him to hold her in his arms and—

The phone started to ring beside her bed. She reached for it. 'Yes,' she said, 'Sara speaking. Who is it?'

'Sara…' Anger went through her as she heard her stepfather's voice. 'Please, don't hang up on me. I must talk to you…please!'

'I thought I'd made it plain I didn't want to speak to you.'

'Please just give me a chance. Your aunt gave me your number—'

'She had no right!'

'Please, listen, Sara.' His voice had a humble, pleading note that made her hesitate before banging the receiver down, as she was tempted to do. 'I showed Mary Rose's diary. She believes me…she believes I'm innocent. I wouldn't have had an affair while Rose was ill. I just wouldn't have done that to her. I cared about her—just as I care about you. Why can't you believe me?'

'Why was Mum so convinced you were cheating on her? She said you were always making excuses about being late. Why would she say things like that if they weren't true?'

'I wish I knew,' he said, sounding miserable. 'Unless

it was because she was so ill. She was jealous of everyone those last months, Sara, even you—it's all in her
diary. I wasn't going to say anything because I didn't
want to hurt you, but you're so unreasonable—'

'How dare you?' Sara was enraged. 'Don't you ever
ring me again!'

She slammed the receiver down and began to shake as
the memory of her mother's still, white face came back
to haunt her. Peter had always maintained that he hadn't
been having an affair. He hadn't come to the hospital that
night because he hadn't been able to stand seeing Rose
in so much pain, and had gone to a pub to deaden his
grief.

But nothing could change the fact that Rose had died
calling for him and in more pain than she'd needed to
be, Sara thought bitterly, her throat catching as the agony
of that time returned to haunt her.

Damn Peter for calling her! Damn him for calling tonight, just as she was beginning to think she might be
able to put the past behind her. How could she when her
beloved mother had suffered so much because of what
Peter had done?

Sara had always liked her stepfather. She'd trusted
him, even loved him once, accepting him as the father
she'd lost—and the discovery that he'd cheated on her
dying mother had helped destroy her faith in all men.

But supposing she'd misjudged Peter? Supposing her
mother's accusations had been the rambling of a sick
woman's mind?

Yet why would Rose have convinced herself of his
guilt if it hadn't been true? Sara couldn't believe she
would have done such a thing…which meant that her
stepfather was lying to cover his own guilt.

And if he couldn't be trusted, a man she had adored as a child, what man could?

Richard was kept busy with calls that night. His first came five minutes after he got back to the cottage.

The first call was to a man who'd been drinking and had fallen down the stairs. He'd twisted his back and was in a lot of pain, though he seemed to have escaped serious injury. Richard sent him to the A and E unit at St Saviour's for further investigation.

His second call came through on the mobile before he returned to the cottage. Mrs Ross had phoned to tell him that her husband had been having severe chest pains all afternoon. Richard's examination had led him to think that it might be a mild heart attack. He put through an urgent call to the hospital, asking them to be ready to take an emergency patient.

He did his best to calm both Mrs Ross and the patient, telling them that everything was going to be all right. By calling him so promptly, he believed they'd avoided the worst scenario, and promised he would visit both his patient and Mrs Ross the next day. After seeing the anxious couple into the ambulance, Richard managed to get back to the cottage and snatch a coffee before the next call came through. This time it was for an elderly man who was vomiting and experiencing chest pains.

It sounded as if he, too, might be suffering a mild heart attack, but after examining him thoroughly Richard decided it was merely a nasty case of the dreaded flu bug. He gave him some antibiotics which would not touch the flu virus, but would help the patient fight the bronchitis which had developed as a secondary infection.

He had three more calls before they suddenly tailed off. One was a diabetic child who had gone into a coma and needed immediate hospitalization, the other two were both suffering from flu.

It was no wonder Jack and his partners needed someone to cover for them if this was their usual workload, Richard thought as he took a shower at eight o'clock on Sunday morning. No one could stay up all night and all day too often. Even he was beginning to feel a little groggy.

However, an invigorating shower soon put him right. He drank strong black coffee and went to raid his friend's wardrobe for warm clothes.

Right at the very back of the hall cupboard was a rather scruffy-looking sheepskin jacket. Just right for what he had in mind. He pulled on a polo-neck sweater of his own and dug out a scarf from Jon's college days, then looked at himself in the mirror and grinned.

There wasn't much of the rarefied atmosphere left about him now. He wouldn't buy a second-hand car from himself, looking the way he did at this minute, but it was exactly what he needed for his date with Sara.

It was bitterly cold outside. The Range Rover's windscreen was white with frost, though it had just begun to thaw. He turned the key in the ignition, thankful that it started at once. Despite the way it looked, it had never let him down yet.

It was a small meeting, just as Sara had said, but about fifty supporters had turned up to cheer the riders on as they careered madly over the rough terrain. To Richard it looked like a muddy waste ground, but apparently the various slopes, ditches and bumps were what made it fun.

There wasn't a refreshment tent or even a hot-dog stand, but most people had come prepared with flasks and picnics. Sara had brought a hamper for them to share with Chris and his friend.

'A lot of it was left over from the party,' she explained. 'But I did make some fresh cheese rolls, and there's coffee or tea if you get cold, standing about.'

'What about you?'

'Oh, I shan't be cold. I'm riding Chris's second bike.'

He'd guessed as much when she'd come out to the car wearing her leathers. A new set, he'd noticed, not the ones she'd torn the night she'd come off the bike and gone into a ditch.

Richard wished her good luck, frowning slightly as she went off to prepare for the first race. He felt a bit as if he'd been deserted, but that soon turned to apprehension as he watched Sara compete. He was scared to death as he saw the way the bikes skidded and bumped over the rough track, and relieved when it ended.

Sara didn't win, but she came in a creditable third. She was laughing when she ran back to him, her helmet off and her hair swinging loose.

'What did you think? Did you enjoy it?'

'I thought you were all mad,' Richard said. 'It frightened the life out of me, Sara. I was certain you would come off and hurt yourself.'

'Scaredy cat,' she cried, her eyes sparkling with excitement. 'It's less dangerous than riding on the road. People come off all the time, but hardly anyone ever gets hurt.'

'What if someone did?' Richard asked, his eyes narrowed and thoughtful. 'At a meeting like this, you have no medical stand by to help in an emergency.'

'Of course we do,' Sara scoffed. 'I'm a nurse and you're a doctor—what more do we need?'

'Quite a few things if there was a nasty accident.'

'There won't be,' Sara said. 'I promise. So stop worrying, Richard. If you'd ever ridden a bike you wouldn't think it was dangerous.'

'I have,' Richard said, frowning. 'Years ago. A friend of mine cut in front of a car one wet night. He was knocked off his bike and died of his injuries a few hours later. I was there when it happened, a short distance behind him—and at the hospital.'

Sara's teasing laughter died instantly. 'I'm so sorry, Richard. I didn't realize. This must be painful for you…'

'No, not painful. Just a bit nerve-racking. I wouldn't want anything to happen to you, Sara.'

'You're really nice to care about me,' she said, then reached up to kiss him briefly on the mouth. He resisted the temptation to hold her closer, merely touching her cheek with his fingertips. 'We could leave if you like.'

She looked so beautiful, so alive and happy, as if the racing had somehow helped her shed the shadows that sometimes hung over her. How could he spoil things for her by inflicting his own anxieties on her? Of course he couldn't!

'And spoil your day? No, I'll stick it out, Sara. I suppose I'll get used to it after a while.'

'I'll be careful,' she promised. 'Please, don't be anxious. Nothing is going to happen to me.' She flashed him a brilliant smile that made him catch his breath. 'Sorry. I have to leave you again now.'

In the second race, Sara shot into the lead on the third lap. Up until then, Richard had been apprehensive, but all of a sudden he found himself cheering her on. She certainly had guts! When she won easily, he was elated.

'I thought you were going to be careful?' he said, grinning at her when she came back. 'But you were great anyway.'

Sara laughed and threw her arms about his waist. 'Wasn't I brilliant?' she cried. 'It's always safer out front, Richard. It's when you get in a tangle with the slower riders that you can come a cropper.'

Richard enjoyed the hug. It took all his will-power not to crush her in a passionate embrace. He joined in her excitement, realizing he'd been silly to worry. This was a muddy field, not a busy road on a wet night.

'So what happens next?' he asked.

'I've got two more heats, then the final,' Sara said. Her eyes searched his face. 'Feeling better about things now?'

'Much.' Richard stamped his feet to keep out the cold. 'Want some coffee before you go get them, champ?'

Sara smiled but shook her head. 'When it's over,' she said. 'Look, why don't you sit in the car for a while? Your hands are frozen.'

'I *am* frozen,' he replied with a grimace. 'But I'm not going to miss your races.'

'Chris is in the next heat,' she said. 'I shan't beat him—he's too good. But I only need to come third in my next two heats to be in the final.'

Richard nodded. He poured some coffee, watching as the next heat began. Chris shot into the lead and stayed there. Sara came in third. She was fourth in her last heat, but scraped into the final as the best of the losers.

Seeing how much she was enjoying herself, Richard began to relax. A few riders had come off, but none of them seemed bothered. They simply picked themselves up and got back on their bikes to finish the race.

Richard watched the final with rising excitement. Despite his misgivings, he had to admit it did give the spectators a rush of adrenaline.

Chris led from the beginning, but Sara got a start on the others and was hot on her cousin's tail. Then Chris suddenly hit something—a bit of wood or debris that had been churned up out of the ground during earlier races. His bike shot into the air and turned over, trapping him beneath it as he and the bike slid across the ground, twisting and turning and rolling over until it came to an abrupt stop against an iron post that had been put up to mark the route.

Sara's bike swerved as she braked. She let it slide from under her and went rushing to her cousin's side. Richard saw her bend over him, then she was on her feet, waving her arms frantically in his direction.

Fortunately, someone had had the sense to stop the race. Richard ran across the track. He was already afraid that Chris's accident was serious.

'He's hurt…' Sara was frightened. He sensed her panic. 'I think it's his head…'

Richard knelt beside the rider. Chris was lying very still. He'd hardly moved since he'd smashed into the post.

'Careful,' Richard warned as Sara undid the straps of Chris's gloves. 'Don't move him until I've checked him over.'

'I was going to feel for a pulse.'

'He's still breathing,' Richard said. He lifted the helmet visor. 'But there's blood on his face. I think he hit his head on the post.' He took his mobile phone from his jacket pocket. 'You'd better ring for the ambulance. You know exactly where we are.'

Chris had started to make faint moaning noises. He opened his eyes and looked at them, then swore and tried to sit up.

'Stay there for a moment,' Richard said. 'Just until the ambulance comes.'

'Damn the ambulance' Chris pushed the other man's

hands away and sat up. He removed his helmet, revealing a jagged but not deep cut on his forehead. There was a dent in his helmet, but it had undoubtedly saved him from a more severe injury. 'I'm all right. Don't bother with an ambulance, Sara. I'll get Terry to drive me to hospital. They'll patch me up.'

Richard gave him a clean handkerchief, which he pressed to the cut on his forehead.

'You'll need a few stitches in that cut,' he said. 'If your friend will look after the bikes, I'll take you up to A and E myself.'

'I'll stay and help with the bikes,' Sara said. 'Go with Richard, Chris. You ought to make sure there's nothing else wrong. Just to be safe.'

'You can talk!' Chris muttered, clearly annoyed at all the fuss. When he got to his feet he suddenly swayed and looked as if he felt a bit light-headed. 'All right, then. Tell Terry to drop you off and then take the bikes home.'

'Your cousin is right,' Richard said. 'You were concussed briefly. You need to be properly checked out in hospital.'

'Oh, for goodness' sake, stop fussing.'

Chris glared at them both, but was feeling too groggy to walk on his own. He allowed Richard to help him across to the parked cars. His face was white as he got into the Range Rover.

Sara watched them go. She was still feeling sick. For a moment she'd been afraid that her cousin was badly injured. She would have liked to have gone with them to the hospital, but there wasn't really any need—and Chris wouldn't have gone if she hadn't agreed to stay and take care of his precious bikes.

It took about an hour to pack everything up, and then another before she was back at the house she shared with her friends. She checked the answerphone, thinking that Richard might have rung to let her know how her cousin was. A light was flashing, but when she pressed the play button it was Peter again.

'Please, Sara, let me come and see you. Let me show you Rose's diary and her letter to me. You must believe me. I never—'

Sara switched the machine off and went to make herself a coffee. She was in no mood to think about Peter's request at this moment.

Why hadn't Richard phoned? Was Chris worse than she'd thought? He might have had a relapse—accident victims didn't always present all their symptoms at first.

She drank her coffee, then made herself another. Damn Richard! Why hadn't he phoned? He was the same as all the rest—thoughtless and careless of others' feelings. She would be mad to trust him.

She paced the sitting-room floor, nearly going out of her mind. Why didn't someone phone?

Sara rushed to the door as she heard a car draw up outside. She opened the door as Richard got out and came up the path towards her, flinging it wide.

'Why didn't you ring?' she asked, her eyes stabbing at him accusingly. 'I've been worried all this time.'

'I didn't have your number,' Richard said. 'It's all right, Sara. Chris was lucky this time. It could have been much worse, as I'm sure you know.'

'Yes, of course.' She chewed her bottom lip nervously. 'Nothing like that has ever happened before. We've both come off during racing but neither of us has been hurt until today.'

'Accidents do happen in sport, Sara.'

'Yes, I know. Where's Chris?'

'They're keeping him in for observation—you know

it's routine after something like that bang on the head. He seems OK, but there could be internal swelling or bleeding. No sign of it yet, though. I don't need to explain the risks to you, do I?'

Sara shook her head. 'No, I've been thinking about it while I was waiting for you. I was terrified when he slid into that post so hard. For a moment I thought he might be dead.'

'He could have been…or he could have had brain injuries,' Richard said. 'That's why I want you to consider giving up riding the bikes, Sara. Why not take up something marginally safer, like kick-boxing or hockey?'

The teasing note in his voice made her laugh. It sounded as though he really cared and that made her feel warm inside. She gazed up into his eyes, feeling the now familiar pull on her heart. This man was special, unlike any she'd known before.

'It's just that it was something I shared with Chris,' she said, 'and it's fun. I've never thought about the dangers until now.'

She suddenly discovered she was trembling. Delayed shock, of course. The sight of her cousin lying there like a rag doll had terrified her. She sat down on the sofa with a little bump as her legs went weak.

'You could do with a drink,' Richard said. 'Have you got anything?'

'There's wine in the fridge…or some whisky over there.' She glanced towards the rather ugly sideboard. 'Maureen keeps it for colds. I can't stand the taste.'

'Nevertheless, it might be a good idea.'

Richard opened the sideboard and took out the bottle and a glass.

'Drink it down in one go,' he commanded, and she obeyed.

Richard sat on the lumpy sofa beside her. He put his arm around her, drawing her close so that her head was leaning on his shoulder. He bent his head to kiss her hair.

Sara stiffened. She didn't want to, but she couldn't quite stop herself.

'It's OK,' he said softly. 'Just relax, Sara. Let yourself go. You're quite safe with me. I just want to make you feel better. I'm not going to jump on you.'

'I know.' She gave a laugh that might have been a sob. 'It's just that most men do if I give them the chance.' One man had done so much more, hitting her across the face so hard that her lip had bled and she'd had black eyes for a couple of weeks. And just because she'd said no—because she'd fought back when he'd tried to force her!

Richard kissed her hair again. 'Someone hurt you, didn't they? Do you want to talk or just stay close?'

'Just stay close,' Sara said in a soft, whispery voice. 'It's nice like this, Richard…'

'Yes, very nice.'

She liked the feel of his arm around her. She was warm and her body relaxed, instinctively recognizing that it was safe to do so. She was aware that being close to Richard was easing the ache she'd carried inside her, the human contact something she'd needed without knowing it for a long, long time.

They sat like that, without talking, for ages. Sara became aware that Richard had closed his eyes. The hours spent in that cold, wet and muddy field had taken its toll of him. She smiled as his head came down on her shoulder and she realized that he'd actually fallen asleep.

She sensed that it had been a long time since he'd been this close to another person, and that he needed this sleep. He'd told her that he didn't sleep much, but he'd been working all hours recently, and the cold air and exercise had caught up with him.

He didn't stir as she very carefully left the sofa. She eased his legs out so he was resting more comfortably, then placed a cushion beneath his head and a blanket over him. Then she bent down and kissed him very gently on the lips.

He murmured a name in his sleep. Beth—the name of the girl he'd told her had died.

Was he still haunted by the tragedy? Did he still love her?

Sara turned away sadly. Why did things have to be so complicated?

When Richard woke it was late. He was lying on the old sofa. Someone had placed cushions behind his head and a blanket over his legs. Just one small shaded lamp was burning somewhere behind him.

He sat up, then glanced at his watch and swore beneath his breath. It was past eleven! He had slept for almost six hours.

'Feeling better?'

Sara's teasing voice made him glance towards a door that apparently led into the kitchen. She was carrying two mugs of coffee, which she brought over and set on the little table in front of him.

'Sorry,' Richard apologized. 'I don't remember ever having done that to a girl before. It was rude of me. I just felt so relaxed…and warm.'

'Poor Richard,' Sara said. 'You aren't used to getting frozen. At least, I hope it wasn't the company that sent you to sleep?'

He saw that she thought it was funny and grinned at her. 'I shall never get you to take me seriously now,' he said, then suddenly remembered. 'Damn! I was supposed to be on call three hours ago.'

'It's all right,' Sara said. 'There's no need to worry. When I realized you were fast asleep I rang your brother-in-law. He told me to let you sleep, said he'd cover for you and you could make it up another time.'

Richard pulled a rueful face. 'It was because I could see that Jack was working far too hard that I offered to do this job in the first place. Now he's having to cover for me.'

'You were obviously tired,' Sara said. 'I'm sure Dr Harper won't mind. He was quite insistent that I should let you sleep on as long as you needed to. Oh—and Angela sent her love and hoped you'd visit her soon.'

Richard nodded and sipped his coffee. Trust his sister to place the wrong interpretation on him being asleep on Sara's sofa. No doubt he would get the third degree when he next saw her. He stretched and yawned. The rest had done him good. He felt surprisingly better for it.

'Then it only leaves an apology due to you, Sara.'

'You can take me out to lunch one day to make up for it,' she said. She wasn't in the least put out that he'd fallen asleep when he was supposed to be comforting her. She was a truly amazing woman! 'I'm working days for a couple of weeks, but my day off is on Tuesday.'

'I'm on permanent nights for the time being,' Richard said, 'though I get one night off midweek. Lunch sounds good. Tuesday, then?'

'Yes, I think so—but in case something comes up and you can't make it, you'd better have this,' Sara said. She thrust a small piece of paper at him. 'My telephone number. Call me?'

'Yes, I will.' Richard finished his coffee. 'Soon.'

He leaned towards her. She was very still as he bent

to kiss her, but she didn't move away. Richard's mouth brushed hers in the softest of kisses. He didn't attempt to deepen the caress or to hold her in his arms, though he wanted to very much. He looked deep into her lovely eyes, which seemed to want to trust him but reflected her doubts.

'We'll talk about it one day,' he said softly. 'When you're ready, Sara. I think there's something you might want to tell me—isn't there?'

'Yes.' Her eyes misted with tears, but she blinked them away resolutely. 'It isn't you, Richard. Believe me. I wish…' She shook her head. 'I will tell you. I promise…'

He touched a finger to her lips. 'Let's get to know each other a little more, Sara. When you're ready to trust me, I'll be here for you.'

The flu was still claiming its victims, Sara noticed as she went on duty next morning. There were two more serious cases, which had been brought in overnight. One was a woman in her early sixties. She was complaining of severe chest pains.

Sara checked her patient's vital signs several times that morning, feeling worried when she noticed a sudden drop in her blood pressure and some breathlessness. She suspected a mild heart attack and sent for the doctor on call. He confirmed her suspicions and ordered the appropriate medication for her and oxygen to help with her breathing.

'That was well spotted, Sister Linden,' he said. 'Keep an eye on her and call me again if you notice anything untoward.'

The other new patient was an elderly man whose bronchitis had led to complications. The doctors had thought there might be some fluid in his lungs and had written up a course of antibiotics, but it was necessary to keep a watch in case it turned to pneumonia.

The day shift was always busy. There was so much to get through—doctors' rounds, visits from the physio-therapist, very necessary if patients were to keep their mobility during long periods of inactivity. There were patients going for X-rays and treatment, coming back from operations after a stay in Intensive Care. That was beside all the bedpans, baths and bed-making that made up the routine of hospital life.

Mrs Reed was having difficulty doing her insulin in-jections herself. It was something she needed to get used to before she could go home. Sara had already spent an hour showing her, but it was necessary to go through the whole procedure again.

'I'm such a silly old thing,' she said. 'I can't quite get it right.'

'You're not silly,' Sara reassured her. 'Injecting your-self isn't easy for anyone. There might be an alternative. I'll speak to doctor about it.'

There were several new devices on the market now, which made the daily chore of administering insulin much easier, but they weren't always suitable, and she didn't want to raise Mrs Reed's hopes until she'd checked with the doctor in charge of her case.

It was noon before Sara had time to phone the hospital at King's Lynn and enquire about her cousin. She was told he'd discharged himself that morning.

It was too bad of Chris, Sara thought. He really shouldn't have done it. Every doctor and nurse frowned on a patient discharging himself because it could be dan-gerous.

Chris wouldn't even have gone to A and E in the first place if it hadn't been for Richard, Sara thought, a little

smile playing about her mouth as she recalled the way
he'd fallen asleep on her shoulder the previous evening.

He'd looked so gorgeous when he'd been asleep, his
hair falling across his brow and a slight six-o'clock
shadow on his chin.

It had made him seem a little vulnerable, and had
reached her heart in a way she hadn't thought possible.
She would have liked to have touched him as he'd slept,
but she'd been afraid of disturbing him.

She sighed, glancing at her watch and wondering what
he was doing right now.

She would have liked to have telephoned him at home,
but thought he might be sleeping. It was going to be
awkward for a while now. With Richard on nights and
Sara on days, they wouldn't get to see much of each
other. And if he was thinking of leaving the area soon,
that might be the end of any relationship between them,
even though he'd said he wanted them to get to know
each other more. What could she believe?

Sara realized she would miss Richard if she didn't see
him again. But of course she would. They were having
lunch the next day…

CHAPTER SEVEN

THERE was a letter lying on the mat in the hall when Richard went downstairs that Monday morning. It had a Manchester postmark. He opened it, frowned and tossed it aside. They were sorry not to be able to offer an interview as the post had already been filled.

He'd applied for two positions he'd seen advertised in the *British Medical Journal,* one in Manchester, the other in London. He had not yet received a reply to the application for the London post.

His preference was, in any case, for the position in London, so he wasn't too disappointed to learn that the job in Manchester had gone. His brother-in-law had told him that weekend that they'd come to an agreement over their new partner, who would be joining them in a month's time.

Richard had thought long and hard, and had come to a decision to accept Jonathan's offer.

He rang his office after making and eating a substantial breakfast. Jonathan was delighted.

'That's wonderful news, Richard. I know my partners will be delighted that you're going to join us—even on a part-time basis.'

'I'm thinking of two consecutive days a week,' Richard said. 'And I'll stay overnight so we can schedule early mornings and evenings, whichever suits your patients.'

'I'll have the contract drawn up. When do you want to start operating?'

'From the beginning of March,' Richard said. 'Or when you think you will have work for me.'

'I've already had enquiries,' Jonathan replied. 'I mentioned the possibility of you joining us to some clients of mine who are wanting a good plastic surgeon for their injured daughter. I'm sure we'll continue to add more challenging, non-cosmetic cases once we have your name on our list but your first jobs are likely to include some straightforward cosmetic work.'

'Don't your partners need to interview me?' Richard asked, amused by his friend's enthusiasm.

'We'll do that by way of a luncheon party,' Jonathan said. 'A week next Sunday at my place. Come and meet everyone.'

'Thanks, I will,' Richard said. 'Can I bring someone?'

'Don't tell me there's romance in the air?'

'She's just a friend, Jon,' Richard said. 'You know her—Sara Linden. We met at your New Year's Eve party.'

There was a brief silence, then Jonathan said, 'Bring Sara, by all means, Rich. She will probably be bored, they're all pretty staid types, but she'll be welcome.'

'Don't worry,' Richard said dryly. 'She won't wear anything provocative. Sara knows how to behave when she wants to.'

'Of course. I didn't mean…'

'Of course not. We'll see you on Sunday.'

Richard was frowning as he replaced the receiver. He was aware of feeling anger on Sara's behalf, yet he knew her behaviour at the New Year's Eve party had left her vulnerable to criticism. Even so, he wouldn't stand for her being slighted. If Jonathan and his partners weren't prepared to accept Sara, he might have to reconsider working with them.

If they were going to have a relationship, Sara must be able to feel comfortable in his world. He'd gone along with her love of dancing and motorcross, though he would be much happier if she stuck to watching the latter, and he wanted her to enjoy the things he liked—walking, swimming and the theatre, as well as classical music and books. She would need to at least share some of his enthusiasms if they were going to stand a chance in the future.

From his experiences in the past, Richard had learned that physical attraction wasn't enough. A couple needed mutual liking and understanding to survive the rigours of modern living—especially with a job like his, which meant he might have to work unsociable hours.

Was he seriously thinking of taking things that far? Richard considered, then realized that somewhere along the line he'd gone beyond having a choice. He didn't know where their relationship might be heading, but he did know there was a mutual attraction.

He wasn't sure just when his interest had become more than mere concern for a young woman he'd sensed was in need of love and kindness. Had it been when she'd come off her bike the first time, when he'd been so anxious after she'd fainted twice? Or when that lout had hit her in A and E and he'd had to force himself to remember that he was there to treat patients and not to murder them? Or the first moment he'd seen her on New Year's Eve?

He hadn't known that within the space of a few weeks his feelings for her would have become so strong. But the realization that he wanted to make love with her had been growing for a while.

And that was something he must hide from Sara, at least for the moment. He'd known almost from the beginning that, far from being the type of girl who slept around, she was afraid of being involved in a sexual re-lationship.

Sara was tired when she came off duty that evening. She hadn't been sleeping well these last couple of nights, and it had been a hectic day on the wards, though it looked as though the flu cases were beginning to tail off and some absentees were returning to work.

The worst thing of all was that she'd discovered that Mr Ross had died in Intensive Care of a heart attack. Apparently, he'd been sent in late on Saturday with what had been thought to be a mild attack, but had had another massive one during Sunday afternoon.

Sara remembered the couple, how neat and nice their cottage had looked the day she'd called, and the love she'd felt between them. It was so very, very sad. She wondered what Mrs Ross would do now. She could hardly go on living in that cottage alone. Her husband had worried about her so much, and now she was the one left behind. It was odd the way that happened sometimes.

Sara sighed as she let herself into the house she shared with Maureen and Phyllis, feeling pleased as she heard sounds coming from the kitchen. At least one of her friends was home. Then Phyllis came out dressed in a brand-new outfit and Sara's heart sank. Phyllis was ob-viously on her way out.

'Heavy date?' she asked, wondering why the thought of spending the evening alone seemed so unappealing. She'd always quite enjoyed having the place to herself for a while.

'Yes—special boyfriend,' Phyllis said. 'I went shop-ping today so there's plenty of stuff in the fridge. Help yourself to whatever you want. It was my turn to stock up anyway.'

'Thanks…'

Sara smiled as she watched her friend disappear through the front door. She went to investigate the fridge, discovered some yogurt and sweet, seedless grapes and took a bunch into the sitting room with her.

She switched on the TV, then switched it off again, feeling restless. She'd just finished eating when she heard a car pull up outside and then her doorbell rang.

She went to answer it, her heart beating very fast as she saw Richard standing there. He was carrying a bag that, if the smells issuing from it were anything to go by, contained a Chinese take-away.

'I saw your car as I was on my way to get a meal,' he said, smiling at her. 'I've arranged for any calls to come through on my mobile for the rest of the evening, so I thought we could share this. Unless you were about to go to bed?'

'No, not just yet,' she said, her spirits rising. 'I've had my tea, but I don't mind picking at a few bits while you eat. And I'll be glad of some company. I heard this evening that Mr Ross died. We had him on the ward after his operation, and I got to know and like both him and his wife. I can't help wondering what she'll do now.'

'I went to see her this afternoon. Her son and daughter are staying at the cottage, helping her sort things out. I'm sure she'll go and live with one of them when it's all settled.'

'Yes, I suppose so—but they were so comfortable and happy when I visited. I can't believe it happened. He seemed so well.'

'I suppose the operation was a great strain,' Richard said. 'But I thought it was a mild attack when I sent him in—I was as shocked by the news as you are. But these things happen sometimes.'

'Well, are you going to eat something?' Sara asked, making an effort to lighten the atmosphere. 'We can't talk shop all night or that food will get cold.'

Richard looked at the yogurt pot and grape stalks and frowned. 'You don't eat enough to keep a sparrow alive,' he said. 'There's far more than I want here so you can help me out—OK?'

'OK,' Sara said, and laughed. 'As a matter of fact, that smells so good I'm beginning to feel hungry.' She moved towards the kitchen. 'I think we have a bottle of wine open—or would you prefer fizzy water?'

'Water for me, I'm on call,' Richard said, his eyes warm and caressing as they followed her. 'I may get called out before we've finished eating, but they don't usually start until later. When any sensible person is tucked up in bed and fast asleep.'

Sara laughed. She was feeling so much better already, her tiredness slipping away as if it had never been, but, of course, it wasn't really her work that had made her feel so low, though the death of a patient she liked had upset her. Deep down she knew it was the knowledge that she'd begun to feel something more than friendship for this man, and it was the uncertainty about where their relationship was heading that was playing on her mind.

She'd felt that it couldn't possibly go anywhere much. Richard hadn't shown any sign of being interested in more than being friends, which was her fault, of course. She'd kept him at arm's length the whole time, so she couldn't expect him to declare he was passionately in love with her. Yet now he was here with her, smiling, making her laugh, filling her life with the kind of happiness that had been missing for too long, and suddenly

all she wanted to do was to relax and enjoy being with
him.

Somehow her inhibitions seemed to have melted away.
As Richard sat on the sofa, Sara squatted on the carpet
at his feet, passing the cartons of tasty, spicy food between them.

They talked all the time, with their mouths full, laughing, teasing and spluttering as they had to swallow hard
because the food went down the wrong way. It was as if
they had known each other for ages, their excitement at
catching up with all the things they both liked spilling
out as for the first time Sara really opened up.

Richard didn't ask any questions, he was just letting
her talk, and Sara was grateful. She'd already told him
her mother had died of cancer and he'd expressed his
understanding of her grief. Sara drew a deep breath, sens-
ing that this was the time to tell him about the way her
mother had died...about the pain and feelings of betrayal
her stepfather's behaviour had aroused, which had led to
her distrust of men in general. And perhaps then she
might be able to speak of the attempted rape, which had
blighted her love life ever since.

'Richard...' she began. 'There's something I need to
tell you...'

'Yes, I know,' he said. 'I've felt there was something
on your mind for a while now. Take your time, Sara.
There's no rush, we have all the time in the world.'

All the time in the world. Sara laid down her food
carton and moved forward onto her knees. She wanted to
explain, she wanted to tell him what was in her heart.

'Oh, damn!' she exclaimed as the front doorbell rang.
'I suppose I shall have to answer that...'

She gave him a rueful look, then got to her feet and

went to the door, opening it wide. As she saw who was standing there, she gasped with dismay.

'What the hell are you doing here? I don't want to see you—go away!'

'I have to see you. I'm going out of my mind,' Peter Myers said, looking as desperate as he sounded. 'If you don't want my death on your conscience, Sara, you'd better take five minutes to listen to me.'

Sara went cold all over. From the way he looked, he might just be desperate enough to do what he'd just threatened. She stood back reluctantly, allowing him to enter.

'Is something wrong, Sara?'

Richard had got to his feet and was looking at her oddly.

'This is my stepfather,' Sara said, her tone harsh, cold. 'He insists on seeing me...'

'Do you want me to stay?' Richard asked.

'I need to talk to you alone,' Peter said. 'Please, Sara.'

'No.' She raised her head, looking into his eyes. 'You asked for five minutes. So don't waste them.'

'I've brought you Rose's diary,' Peter said. 'And a letter she wrote to me a day or so before she died. Read them, Sara, that's all I ask. You judged me from what she said to you that night. You found me guilty without a trial, without listening to my side of things. I wouldn't have shown you these if you'd been willing to listen. I don't want to hurt you—but this isn't fair.'

'I don't want to listen to you. It's your fault she's dead...you hurt her so badly. You caused her so much grief...' Sara cried, and burst into tears. 'I hate you. I hate you!'

'What's going on here?' Richard asked, moving towards her protectively. 'Do you want me to get rid of him, Sara?'

'I never meant to hurt Rose,' Peter said, his voice catching with emotion. 'I cared for her. Maybe we weren't in love towards the end, but we were happy enough. I just couldn't stand to see her so ill. I'm a coward, I won't deny that. I should have been with her when she died—but you were there. I thought that was enough.'

Sara's head shot up. 'Of course it wasn't enough. She needed you.'

'I wish I'd been there. I'm sorry. But I couldn't take any more, Sara—the accusations, the guilt, the pain. It was too much.'

'You let her die in pain. She refused the drugs they wanted to give her because she wanted to say goodbye—and you didn't come. You didn't come…' Her voice broke on a sob as she relived the trauma of that evening, alone with her dying mother, praying that Peter would come as the minutes ticked away.

'Yes…' He sighed deeply. 'She wanted to apologize for suspecting me—it's in her letter. She knew she'd been wrong.'

'I don't believe you.'

'Your mother was always jealous, right from the beginning of our marriage—but she was the first to have an affair.'

'No. That's not true.'

'I'm not lying. Read her diary, Sara, then you'll know. It's true I had a friend, but there was nothing between us while Rose lived. I give you my word on that. That night, you accused me of smelling of perfume.' She nodded, and he sighed. 'It was an expression of sympathy from a friend, a hug, that's all.'

'I don't know…I don't know what to believe. I didn't even know Mum was ill until a few weeks before she died. Why did no one tell me anything until it was almost too late?'

'Because you were working so hard, first for your SRN, then to become a sister. Rose was so proud of you. She didn't want you to know she was ill until the last few weeks, that's when her mind began to wander. I think it was the drugs she'd been taking.'

'She should have told me, I might have been able to help.' Sara's mind was reeling as she struggled to come to terms with what he'd just told her. 'It was such a shock…to be told that she was dying, and then discover that you—'

'I didn't do those things she accused me of—please, believe me.'

Dimly, Sara heard Richard's mobile ringing. He answered it, and she knew he had to leave. He came to her as she stood there, her face white, her eyes dark with grief.

'I have to go, Sara,' he said gently. 'It's an emergency. Are you all right? Do you want me to ask him to leave before I go?'

'No…' Sara drew a shuddering breath. She raised her head, her expression proud. 'I can't explain now, but I will another day. Perhaps tomorrow.'

'I might be able to get back…if there aren't too many calls.'

'No, it's all right,' she said, and the tears were beginning to trickle down her cheeks. 'Peter isn't going to hurt me. I think we have to talk. This is something that won't go away, Richard.'

He nodded, then reached out to touch her cheek. 'Yes,

I see that, Sara. I'll leave you to it, then. Take care, my
darling.'

He nodded to Peter, then walked past him and out into
the lane.

Sara took a deep breath, then looked at Peter.

'If what you say is true, I owe you an apology…'

'No, no apologies,' he said huskily. 'I didn't handle
your rejection very well. I've wanted to apologize sin-
cerely for letting both you and your mother down.'

Sara blinked hard as the tears stung her eyes.

'All I could see was Mum's face, the way she held on
just for you,' she said, her throat tight.

'Don't you think that was just as bad for me? Rose
and I were happy most of the time—despite everything.
But she changed once she became ill. She was thoroughly
mixed up inside, Sara. I don't know why she was so
jealous, but if you read the diary you'll see it's true. The
things she says about you—and me—they're not true,
Sara. I love you, but as a daughter. It was never anything
else. I give you my word. For a long time I wasn't going
to let you see this, but I've realized you have to know.
Your mother was very ill. We both have to accept that
the woman she became was not the woman we both
loved. Please, try to understand.'

Sara nodded. She owed him that much.

'All right. I'll read it later. Can I get you something—
coffee?'

'No, thank you. Not this time. I'll leave you to read
the diary, then perhaps we can have lunch or something
one day.'

'Yes…' Sara knew she would have to face up to it
some time. 'Ring me next week. My day off is Tuesday,
but I have a date for tomorrow.'

'With the man who was here when I arrived?'

'Yes—Richard Dalton,' she said. 'We're friends.'

Peter's eyes flicked to the discarded food cartons. 'Just friends, Sara?'

'I'm not sure,' she said, and sighed. 'I don't know whether Richard is planning to be around for ever...'

'But you'd like him to be?'

'I think I might,' she replied. 'I'm waiting to see how things develop.'

'I'm sorry I interrupted.'

'It doesn't matter.'

Peter smiled. 'I hope things turn out well for you.'

'Thank you. So do I.'

Sara saw him to the door, then went back to clear up the remains of the meal. Afterwards, she picked up the diary and letter Peter had left, taking them up to her bedroom to read in bed.

If her mother had really been as mixed up and disturbed as her stepfather said, it made her suspicions and accusations easier to understand. It was very possible that she hadn't meant much of what she'd said, that the fear and pain had affected the balance of her mind.

If only she'd known sooner, if she'd been able to help her mother through the trauma of a terminal illness. But she'd been working away, and no one had told her because they hadn't wanted to upset her.

In the circumstances, it was really no one's fault—just an unfortunate tragedy. She must try to accept it as such, try to put the memories away where they couldn't hurt her.

Sara wasn't sure where Richard would be taking her for lunch, but she imagined it would probably be somewhere nice so she decided to wear a smart black trouser suit and a white silk blouse. She swirled her hair up on top of her head in a sleek chignon, which made her look very sophisticated, and slightly older, then applied a new lipstick in a pretty shade of peach.

She sprayed some of the perfume Richard had given her behind her ears. It really was gorgeous stuff.

Richard came to pick her up at a quarter to twelve as they'd arranged. He was dressed in black trousers, black shirt and tie and a light-coloured suede jacket. Obviously they were going somewhere smart, and Sara was pleased she'd chosen the suit, which was about the most expensive outfit she owned.

'You look lovely, Sara,' he said, his eyes caressing her. 'How are you—no ill effects from yesterday?'

'No.' Sara gave him a shy smile. 'I'm not sure how much you gathered from what Peter said yesterday…'

'Enough to realize you've been going through a bad time,' Richard said, a note of concern in his voice. 'Do you want to tell me about it?

Sara nodded, her throat catching. 'I told you Mum died of cancer—but not the way she died. She refused the injection that would have eased her last hours because she was waiting for Peter to come to say goodbye. He never did…and that tore me apart. I hated him for it.'

'That isn't quite all of it, is it?'

'No. I feel guilty because I didn't realize what was going on. I used to go home for Christmas or holidays, but I thought everything was fine between them. Apparently they'd been quarrelling for a while…and they'd both been seeing other people. My mother's diary confirms that she did have an affair…about four years before she died.'

'You can't blame yourself for what happened, Sara. It was between your parents.'

'Peter says they tried. Apparently, she told him about

the affair and he forgave her, but she felt guilty. She
started to imagine that he was with another woman whenever he was working late. She said he was doing it to
spite her, to pay her back for what she'd done. I think it
must have been pretty rotten for them both.'

'They should have sought professional help.'

'Consulted a marriage guidance counsellor?'

'If necessary, yes.'

'I don't suppose they thought things were that bad—
and then Mum became ill. I think she felt frightened and
it all just got out of hand. But it wasn't just my mother—'

She broke off, and Richard looked at her, his brows
raised.

'What is it you can't bring yourself to say?' Sara was
silent for a moment. 'At a guess I'd say it was something
to do with a man—a man who hurt you in another way?'

'Perhaps…' Sara bit her lip. 'Can we talk about this
later?'

'Yes, of course. But I think you should try to forgive
your stepfather. People do sometimes get things into their
heads—silly things that are just not true.'

He broke off as though he found it too painful to continue.

'Is that what happened to her—the girl you loved?'

'Yes.' He hesitated, then went on, 'She was a model
for a cosmetics firm—very lovely. Then she had a car
accident and her face was scarred. Her father asked me
to do the surgery. I agreed and was able to repair the
worst of the scars. There were two very tiny ones left
after her face had healed.

'Her employers said they made it impossible for them
to use her—but they probably used it as an excuse to
dump her. They went with a new face and a new cam-
paign almost at once. It must have been on the cards

before the accident. Beth thought it was because of the scars. She had no confidence afterwards. I told her they meant nothing to me...'

'But she didn't believe you?'

He nodded, looking thoughtful. 'I had become very fond of her and I asked her to marry me. She was happy for a while, but then...'

Sara gazed up at him, seeing the pain working in his face.

'What happened, Richard?'

'She begged me to do something about the remaining scars. I told her it wasn't necessary—that there were others who needed my skills more than she did...' He turned away. 'She took an overdose of painkillers.'

'Oh, Richard...' Sara felt his hurt. 'I'm so sorry.'

'I blamed myself. I should have listened to her. The scars were important to her. I should have at least tried to help.'

'Is that why you gave up surgery?'

He nodded. 'I watched her die and there was nothing either the other doctors or I could do. It made me lose faith in my profession—in myself. I was overcome with guilt and regret. What was the good of calling myself a doctor when I couldn't even save Beth?'

'We're not gods,' Sara said. 'We can only ever do so much.'

'Yes, I know,' he said, and smiled as if he'd fought his memories and conquered them. 'Anyway, that's enough of confession time. We ought to be leaving.'

'Where are we going?'

'I've heard about a country mansion house where the food is supposed to be terrific,' he said. 'It will take us about half an hour to get there. I thought we would have a leisurely drink in the bar first.'

'Sounds lovely,' Sara said, then reached up to kiss his cheek.

Richard caught her, holding her, his hands loosely about her waist and looking down into her eyes. Then, very deliberately, he lowered his head and kissed her on the lips.

Sara felt the heady sensation sweep over her, a warm, deep desire stirring inside her. She swayed against his body, letting herself relax, enjoying the experience. No man had ever made her feel like this before. She wanted it to go on and on, but Richard was letting her go, smiling as he touched her cheek.

'That was worth waiting for,' he said. 'Shall we go? If we don't leave now we may never get there.'

'I think that was just the most delicious meal I have ever had—that sauce on the salmon was out of this world!' Sara said as they drove home afterwards. 'I've never eaten so much in my life. If we do that often, I shall get fat!'

'It won't hurt you once in while,' Richard said, smiling at her. 'Besides, I don't suppose either of us has the time to lunch out all that often.'

'I've got another week on days,' Sara said, 'then I shall be back on nights. That will make it even more difficult for us to see each other.'

'I shan't be helping out at the practice for long,' Richard said. 'Jack has a new partner starting next month.'

'What will you do after that?' Sara held her breath. Would he say he was going away, leaving England?

'I'm promised to give Jonathan two days a week at his clinic—which means I shall stay over one night.' Richard frowned. 'But I've applied for an NHS position in

London. I would like to split my time between the two…'
He sighed. 'Mind you, I haven't worked for a while. I
may find I've lost my skill.'

'I saw the work you did in A and E on that youth with
a deep cut on his forehead,' Sara said. 'I know how much
neater you were than most of the doctors we get in A
and E. If I ever had an accident and needed my face
stitched, I would rather you did it than anyone else.'

'Thank you,' Richard said, touched by the compliment.
She obviously hadn't had much experience of plastic surgery—or the skill it needed. Skills that only a few surgeons possessed. 'But I would rather you didn't need
patching up in the first place.'

'I have got the message that you think my bike is dangerous,' Sara said with a rueful look in his direction.
'Supposing I needed my nose changed—or my boobs
lifted? Would you make me more beautiful, Richard?'

'You don't need cosmetic work,' he replied, seeming
thoughtful. 'You could do with gaining a couple of
pounds in weight, but otherwise you're perfect.' Sara was
silent but as he spoke again she suddenly remembered
that his refusal to operate on Beth's scars had driven her
to take her own life. 'If you really want something
done…'

Sara went into a peal of delighted laughter. 'First he
tells me I'm perfect, then he reconsiders! No, thanks,
Richard. Anyone who doesn't like me the way I am will
have to put up with it. I've no intention of having my
body carved up for cosmetic reasons.'

'Thank goodness for that,' Richard said, and grinned
at her. 'I wouldn't want to change you, Sara. You look
good to me the way you are.'

'Thank you…' She shot a rather shy glance at him.

They didn't talk much after that. Sara was feeling very

conscious of her own thoughts and desires. She'd known after Richard had kissed her that morning that she wanted to make love with him, but they'd been about to leave for their luncheon appointment. Now they were on their way home, and she couldn't help a flutter of nerves.

She wanted Richard to make love to her, but what would happen when he did? Would she be able to give herself to him…or would she feel revulsion as she had so many times in the past and draw back at the last moment?

'Richard…do you have to leave?' Sara asked when they stopped outside the house. 'Or would you like to come in? I think we'll have the house to ourselves. Phyllis and Maureen are both working.'

'I should like to come in,' Richard said. 'We have the rest of the afternoon, we shouldn't waste it.'

'No…we shouldn't waste it.'

Sara's heart was beating wildly as she unlocked the door and led the way inside. She laid down her shoulder-bag, eased her jacket off and turned to look at him, an expression of appeal in her eyes.

Richard had discarded his jacket. He came towards her, then reached out, drawing her close. He bent his head and kissed her tenderly on the mouth, then with an increasing passion. When he drew away, she had her eyes closed and a look of bliss on her face.

'Richard?' She opened her eyes to look at him. 'Why have you stopped?'

He touched a teasing finger to her mouth. 'I wanted to be sure,' he said. 'I want to make love to you, Sara. I've wanted it for a long time, but I'd rather wait until you're quite sure it's what you want. I think you've had some bad experiences in the past…'

'Yes, I have. One in particular, which was not only frightening but also ended with me having a cut lip and two black eyes. But most of my unhappiness was because of my mother…because I believed…' She shook her head. 'No, that wasn't all of it either—those other men, they just weren't right for me.'

'And you are certain this is right for you? You don't feel I'm rushing things?'

'I want you to make love to me. I care for you, Richard, but in the past I've had to draw back because I lost my nerve at the last moment.'

'You only have to say no and I'll stop.'

'Thank you—but I don't think I'll want to stop.' Sara smiled dreamily. 'Do you think you could kiss me like that again?'

'I think I could.' Richard reached out for her, then frowned as the telephone began to ring. 'I suppose you'd better answer that.'

Sara moved away from him reluctantly. She put the receiver to her ear and listened.

'Auntie Mary. I've been out… What happened?' Sara's face went white. 'When was this? A couple of hours ago. How bad is he?' She gave a little cry of distress. 'Oh, no! That's terrible. I'm so sorry. Yes, of course I'll go. I'll go straight away.'

She turned to look at Richard as she replaced the receiver, her eyes dark with fear.

'It's Chris—he's had a bad accident.'

'That damned bike!'

'No, he wasn't on the bike,' Sara said, and tears welled up in her eyes. 'He was in Terry's truck. Neither of them had been drinking either. Terry wasn't hurt, just bruised—he told my aunt how it happened. A lorry came down the hill and jackknifed on the slippery road. It went straight into them.'

'Where is he?' Richard asked.

'They've taken him to Addenbrookes for emergency surgery. The accident happened on the Cambridge to Royston road. Aunt Mary is trying to get a taxi to take her to the station. She asked if I could meet her at the hospital.'

'I'll take you,' Richard said. 'We'll go straight away, Sara.'

'Oh, Richard, I'm so frightened. If anything happens to him…I can't bear it.'

She ran to him and he put his arms about her as at last she gave in to her tears.

Richard put his lips to her hair. 'It's all right, my darling,' he said. 'It's all right to cry for someone you love.'

'I just can't bear it if he dies…'

'We'll go to the hospital,' Richard said, giving her his handkerchief. 'Don't start imagining things, Sara. Let's hear what they have to say before we give up on Chris.'

'Yes, you're right.' She wiped her eyes, lifting her head proudly. 'He may not be too badly smashed up. We can't tell until we hear what the doctors say.'

CHAPTER EIGHT

RICHARD watched as Sara paced the hospital corridor. It was nearly six o'clock and they'd been waiting for news for over an hour. All they knew so far was that Chris was in Theatre. He had a fracture of his pelvic girdle, a broken rib and some damage to his skull and facial bones.

Sara was right to be anxious, Richard thought. Chris had suffered severe injuries and there could be more—internal injuries that might be more serious than damage to his bones.

He was about to go to her, to try and get her to sit down for a while, when she gave a cry and started to run towards a middle-aged woman who had just come in.

'Auntie Mary!'

'Sara—how is he?'

'Still in Theatre. They haven't told us much.'

Richard watched as the two women embraced. Sara's aunt looked a nice, very ordinary sort of woman with soft brown hair and eyes. He glanced at his watch. He ought to ring Jack, tell him what was going on, that he might be late back that evening.

Sara was bringing her aunt to meet him.

'Auntie—this is Mr Dalton. He's a doctor, a consultant surgeon. We're friends. Richard brought me here as soon as we heard.'

'That was kind of you, Mr Dalton,' Aunt Mary said. 'You must be a busy man—are we keeping you from your work?'

'I hadn't thought…' Sara looked guilty. 'You should go, Richard.'

'Will you be all right with your aunt?' She nodded. He kissed her cheek. 'Then I ought to go. I'll ring St Saviour's and tell them you may not be in tomorrow. I'm sure they'll understand.'

'Yes…' Sara swallowed hard. 'I can't leave my aunt, not while Chris is still in danger.'

'No one would expect it.' Richard smiled at her. 'Ring me when you have news. If I'm out, leave a message. I'll get back to you as soon as I can.' She nodded, he kissed her cheek again, then turned to her aunt. 'Try not to worry. We can do a lot for people in surgery these days.'

Richard felt the wrench as he left the two women to watch and wait. He supposed he could have asked Jack to stand in for him, but that didn't seem fair to his brother-in-law, who'd already taken two heavy surgeries that day.

Sara had her aunt now, and there was nothing Richard could actually do. It was obviously going to be touch and go for a while in there. He was aware of frustration because he wasn't in there, helping to patch Chris up. It was always so much easier when you could do something constructive! Waiting was hell.

'You should have stayed with Sara,' Jack said when Richard told him about the accident a little later that evening. He'd called at the cottage to bring Richard a message from his sister. 'I would have covered for you.'

'I didn't want to ask,' Richard admitted. 'I've asked too much of you already.'

'That's what friendship is for,' Jack said. He wrinkled

his brow in thought. 'Have you decided what you're going to do?'

'I've taken on a part-time commitment to the Rosewell clinic,' Richard said, 'but I'm hoping to do some work for the NHS. There's a job in London I'm interested in, but I haven't heard back from my enquiry yet.'

'I'm glad you've decided to return to surgery,' Jack said. 'I know you needed some time to settle back into routine, but you're wasted as a GP, Richard.'

'Yes, I've begun to think the same way...' Richard smiled ruefully. 'I've realized I need to get back to my own work.'

'It was personal, wasn't it?'

'Yes. Someone I cared about died and I couldn't face the guilt I felt for not being able to save her.'

Jack nodded. 'But now...I think there's someone else. Sara Linden. Am I right?'

Richard smiled. 'Yes. At least, I think we're beginning to get somewhere.'

'Good.' Jack looked pleased. 'Angela has been worried about you. Will you bring Sara for a meal soon?'

'It depends what's happening at the hospital,' Richard said. 'Sara is very fond of her cousin. I expect she'll want to stay with her aunt for a while. Just until things settle down.'

'Yes, of course.' Jack nodded. 'Well, I'll leave you to get on. Angela is expecting me to take her out this evening. By the way, we had a message through to the surgery from a Mr Smith's daughter—apparently you sent him for an emergency operation when you were up at St Saviour's A and E. She rang to say that her father was recovering well, and to thank you for your prompt action in helping to save his life.'

'That's good news—thanks for passing it on.'

Richard made some coffee after Jack left. He wasn't hungry. The meal he'd eaten at lunchtime would see him through until morning. He thought about Sara as he sat in one of the comfortable armchairs in the sitting room. He switched on the music centre and waited for the phone to ring.

It did so half an hour later. Richard was called out to a child of six who had fallen down the stairs. The mother had said he was unconscious, but when Richard arrived, the boy was moaning. His eyes opened spontaneously when he was touched, though he didn't appear to be focusing well.

'Hello, Bobby,' said Richard. 'Can you squeeze my hand?'

The boy's verbal response was disorientated, just incomprehensible words, though his motor response was better. Richard calculated his coma score to be somewhere in the region of eleven. Not good enough to dismiss the fall as harmless, even though his examination of the boy's scalp showed no bruising or swelling as yet.

'I think Bobby should go to A and E for further checks,' he told the child's anxious mother. 'He doesn't seem to have done a great deal of harm, but there could be internal bleeding. I want him to have X-rays and a CT scan.'

'What's a CT scan?'

'It's just a special kind of X-ray really,' Richard explained. 'The X-ray emitter and detector rotate around the patient, which produces a 3-D image. It will highlight brain damage or blood clots.' He saw her look of alarm and immediately reassured her. 'I'm fairly sure Bobby is OK, but we must be certain.'

He telephoned for the ambulance. Bobby seemed to be unhurt physically, but was too dazed for Richard's liking.

He thought it possible there was some intracranial haemorrhaging.

Once the paramedic team arrived, he had a few words in private, then left the patient in their care.

When he got back to the cottage, he saw the green light flashing on the answering machine and rushed over to it.

'It's Sara…' Richard heard the sob in her voice and cursed himself for not being there when she needed him. 'Just to let you know Chris is in the recovery room. The surgeon told us there was no substantial damage to his spine or brain. He does have severe damage to his face. They've patched him up for now, but he's going to need further surgery. It sounds as if the left side of his face will need rebuilding…' Again Sara had to fight her emotion. 'They said he'd been lucky. He could have lost an eye but they managed to save the optic nerve—'

She apparently put the receiver down suddenly, as though she couldn't bear to say any more. Richard wasn't surprised. He would have liked to have called her back, but wasn't sure where she was. He did try phoning her house. Maureen answered on the third ring.

'Do you know where Sara is?' she demanded, obviously anxious.

He explained, asking for her aunt's telephone number. 'Sara rang me, but didn't leave her number. I'd like to contact her.'

'She'll be desperate,' Maureen said. 'Hang on a mo— here's the number you want.' She reeled the digits off. 'If you manage to get her, let me know what's going on, please.'

'Yes, of course I will.'

Richard replaced the receiver then rang the number

Maureen had given him. There was no reply, which meant that Sara was probably still at the hospital.

He ought to have stayed with her! Richard cursed himself for having left her to go through this ordeal alone. There was nothing he could do now, but in the morning he would find out where she was and go to her.

Sara held her aunt's hand as she wept. They'd both been allowed to visit Chris briefly. He was still deeply drugged, his face and head swathed in bandages, but the heart monitor was recording a strong, steady beat and the surgeon had assured them that Chris was out of any immediate danger.

'He's going to be all right,' Sara said. 'The facial injuries were the worst. It will mean operations to restore his cheekbones, but they're fairly certain that there was no lasting brain damage.'

'His poor, poor face,' Mary said. She looked at Sara with anxious eyes. 'It's going to take a long while and a lot of skill to put that right, isn't it?'

Sara couldn't lie to her. 'Yes, I'm afraid it will,' she said. 'I don't know too much about plastic surgery—but I know someone who does. I'll ask Richard to find out more for us. If he speaks to the surgeon who patched Chris up, he'll know what has to be done. Richard worked as a plastic surgeon in America for several years, and I know Jonathan Thirstone was very keen to get him on the staff at the Rosewell.'

'That's your friend, isn't it?' Mary raised her head hopefully. 'Would he operate on Chris himself?'

'I'm not sure that he could,' Sara said. 'He's going into private practice soon, and Chris will have his operations done by the NHS.'

'I want the best for Chris,' Mary said. 'If need be, I'll

pay for him to go private. I've got an insurance policy about to pay out. Speak to Mr Dalton about it, Sara. Please?'

'I'll ask him to have a talk with the doctors here,' Sara said. 'Then we'll see what happens.' She glanced at her watch. 'I'll telephone him now. I didn't want to ring too soon this morning—he was on call all night.'

She went to the telephones in the hospital reception area. Richard answered on the third ring.

'Sara? I've been trying to reach you. I got your message. How is Chris?'

'They say he has no brain damage, but his face is pretty bad, Richard. I wondered if you could have a word with the surgeons here? My aunt is very worried about him.'

'Yes, of course I will,' Richard said. 'Are you staying on at the hospital or going home?'

'We've seen him. He wasn't aware of us, of course. They're keeping him sedated for the moment, so there's not much we can do here. I've rung St Saviour's, told them I shan't be in for a few days. I'm going to take my aunt home in a taxi—shall I give you her phone number?'

'I have that. Maureen gave it to me,' Richard said. 'But if you give me her address again, I'll come over this afternoon. I would fetch you, but you'll be home before I could pick you up.'

Sara gave him the address. 'You remember you took me there the night we first met?'

'Yes, I know—but I wasn't quite sure I remembered the name of the road. I'll be there by three this afternoon, Sara. And I'll have news for you by then.'

'Thank you…' There was a sob in Sara's voice as she replaced the receiver. It was so good to have someone she could trust, someone who understood medicine, who cared how she felt.

Aunt Mary was blowing her nose when she went back to her. She had clearly made an effort to stop crying.

'They've told me they'll let us know when we can visit,' she said. 'I think we should go home, Sara.'

'Yes.' Sara put an arm about her shoulders. 'I've spoken to Richard. He's going to discuss the case with the doctors here, and he'll come to see us this afternoon. Don't worry, Aunt Mary. I'm sure Chris will be all right.'

'You will speak to Mr Dalton about doing the operations himself?'

'I'll see what he thinks,' Sara promised. 'Come on, let's go home—I could do with a bath and something to eat.'

'Oh, Richard...' Sara admitted him into the hall of her aunt's house, then went into his arms, her head against his shoulder as he held her close. 'I'm so glad you're here.'

'I should never have left you last night,' he said.

'No.' She lifted her head, her cheeks stained with tears. 'No, there was nothing you could do—not then. He was already in good hands, and they've been very kind to us.'

'I've checked on the situation,' he said. 'It's going to be a major reconstruction job on his cheekbones, Sara, but nothing I haven't done before. It will mean more than one operation, but in the end Chris shouldn't look too bad. There may be some permanent scarring, of course, but he isn't going to enter any beauty competitions, is he?'

Sara gave a watery laugh. 'What are you saying, Richard? My aunt did say she would pay for Chris to go private if need be—but how much will all this cost?'

'Nothing, as far as my fees are concerned,' Richard
said. 'I've already agreed with Jon that I shall waive
them. We shall have to pay for accommodation at the
Rosewell, naturally—but once I've sold my apartment in
New York that won't be a problem.'

'My aunt wouldn't let you pay for the accommodation,' Sara said. 'She was willing to pay for the surgery,
but I know that might cost ten thousand pounds or more.'

'Chris is entitled to have surgery under the NHS,'
Richard said. 'The work he needs isn't merely cosmetic—but there's a huge waiting list for any work of
this kind. You may know that there are only a handful
of plastic surgeons in the country, and most do private
work as well as their commitment to the NHS.'

'Yes, I do know,' Sara said. 'They need surgeons like
you, Richard.'

He nodded, a slight frown wrinkling his brow. 'Yes,
I've begun to realize that I've wasted too much time already. I shall be glad to start work. And Chris is going
to be my first priority. I've spoken to Jon, and he's agreed
for me to do the first operation as soon as Chris is well
enough to stand it, which should be in a few weeks.'

'I don't know how to thank you,' she said, swallowing
hard.

'You don't have to thank me.' He smiled at her. 'Let's
go and talk to your aunt, Sara. I'm sure she's worrying
more than she needs. There's a risk with all surgery, of
course—but I've done this sort of thing several times in
the past. I believe we can make Chris almost as good as
new.'

'I don't want to leave you alone,' Sara said, looking at
her aunt. 'But I think I should get back to work.'

It had been a week since her cousin's accident, and he

was making good progress. He had been moved out of Intensive Care the previous day and was now in a side ward. When he had recovered sufficiently to leave Addenbrookes, he would be transferred to the Rosewell clinic for the first of his reconstructive operations, but that wouldn't be for a few weeks yet.

'I want you to go,' Mary replied, leaning forward to kiss her cheek. 'I feel so much better since Richard explained everything. He's so kind, Sara. So understanding.'

'Yes, he is,' Sara said, then turned her head as the front doorbell rang. 'That will be Richard now. I'd better not keep him waiting.'

'Run along, then,' her aunt said. 'I've enjoyed having you here, Sara, but I'm all right now. You needn't worry about me any more.'

'I shan't,' Sara replied. 'I know how sensible you are. But if there's anything you need…'

'I'll be in touch,' Aunt Mary said. 'Go on, love. Don't keep your young man waiting.'

Sara laughed at the old-fashioned term. Was Richard her young man? She wasn't sure. He was certainly a good friend—a very caring, considerate man who'd made her feel so much better these past few days.

He'd rung her constantly, and she knew he'd rung the hospital to make his own check on Chris, who was now officially registered as his patient. All the consent forms had been signed, and Richard had made the arrangements for Chris's accommodation at the clinic. He'd wanted to pay all the fees himself but, as Sara had known she would, her aunt had insisted on paying these herself.

Richard smiled as she opened the door to him, a small travel bag in her hand. 'Ready, then?' he asked, and smiled at Aunt Mary as she came to the door of the kitchen.

'Take her home,' Mary said. 'And don't let her fret over me.'

'I shan't,' Richard replied. 'We're going to a luncheon party this weekend, and I'm hoping to persuade her to come to London with me tomorrow.'

'Oh—why?' Sara stared at him in surprise. 'That's the first I've heard of a trip to London.'

'I've been invited for an interview,' Richard said. 'I thought you might like to come with me—go shopping and then meet for lunch? You'll be home in plenty of time for your evening shift.'

Sara didn't start back at St Saviour's until the following evening, so there was no reason why she shouldn't go with him.

'An interview?' she asked. 'In your own field?'

'Yes.' Richard smiled at her. 'They took their time replying, but it was due to some bungle in the administrative chain. Apparently they're quite keen to get hold of me.'

'I should think so, too,' Sara said. She felt a little surge of happiness as she took her seat in his car. 'Does this mean you've given up all idea of returning to America?'

'For the moment,' Richard said. 'I may reconsider in time. I feel they are ahead of us in some ways, and I like to keep abreast of new thinking and techniques, but if the interview goes well, I shall probably stay here for a year or two anyway.'

Sara nodded. She wasn't sure where she came into all this. Richard spoke of perhaps returning to America one day—so where did that leave their relationship?

If, indeed, they had anything more than friendship.

*   *   *

Sara looked at Richard as he stopped the car outside his cottage. She'd been expecting him to take her home and was surprised.

'I thought we could spend the afternoon together,' he said. 'I bought some steaks. I could cook us lunch, if you would like that?'

'Yes, I would,' she said, her heart skipping a beat. Was Richard about to suggest that they take up where they'd left off the day of Chris's accident? 'But you must let me help with the cooking.'

'Another day,' Richard said, his eyes bright with laughter. 'Steak is one thing I'm good at. You can cook for me at your place some time.'

Sara nodded, following him into the cottage. 'This is nice, Richard,' she said, looking about with interest. The furniture was all oak, traditional and fairly ancient. It had a warm, mellow look, the floral curtains and cushions light and attractive. 'Much nicer than our house.'

'Yes, I suppose it is. I hadn't really thought about it— it was just somewhere to stay while I sorted myself out. The sitting room is through there. Pour yourself a drink,' Richard said. 'I'll just have water—there's some ice in the fridge. I'll bring it through.'

'I'll come with you. I want to see what the kitchen is like,' Sara said, following him. She was surprised that, unlike the rest of the house, it was very modern, almost clinical with stainless-steel appliances and surfaces. 'Oh…'

'Jonathan's idea,' Richard said, and laughed. 'I'm not sure I like it, though it's easy to clean. Anyway, I shan't be here much longer. Once I'm settled in my work, I'll look for something more permanent.'

Not wanting him to see the effect that had on her, Sara turned away. He was talking about buying a home somewhere—but where? He was obviously going to need something near a mainline railway station if he was going to commute. They were too isolated here in this part of Norfolk, too far down winding, twisting lanes to make viable a regular journey backwards and forwards to London.

So where did that leave them? She was just beginning to feel that Richard was important to her, but hadn't she always known he would be going away before too long? She took the ice bucket he handed her and went through to the sitting room, pouring them both fizzy water over ice.

When she returned to the kitchen, Richard was tossing the salad he'd taken from the fridge and the steaks were browning on the griddle.

'I hope you like the dressing,' Richard said. 'It's my own recipe.' He took the glass from her and sipped, then frowned. 'Something wrong, Sara?'

'No, of course not…' She sighed, then realized she couldn't keep her feelings inside. 'I was just thinking I'll miss you when you go to London.'

'Ah…' Richard nodded in understanding. 'I realize it may be a problem. But I'm sure we can solve it.'

'Yes, I expect so.'

Sara wanted to say more but the phone was ringing. Richard pulled a face then went out into the hall to answer it. She could hear his side of the conversation quite plainly.

'Kurt! How long will you be in London? I'm coming up tomorrow for an interview.' Richard's voice sounded wary. 'Lunch. No, I couldn't manage that tomorrow. Sorry. Maybe on Friday. You can't make that?'

There was a longish silence, then he said, 'I hadn't considered coming back. Not for the time being. No, I think I'll settle here for the moment. Look, I really can't talk now. I'm sorry, I have to go. I have someone here…'

Richard came back to the kitchen. Sara was turning the steaks, which had started to burn.

'I'm sorry about that,' he said. 'It was someone I knew in America. He's staying in London for a couple of days and wanted me to meet him tomorrow. Apparently, he's going back the day after.'

'You should have told him you would meet him tomorrow,' Sara said. He obviously hadn't wanted to talk to his friend with her listening, and it made her wonder. 'I wouldn't have minded, Richard. I don't have to come with you tomorrow. I have things to do…'

His eyes narrowed as he looked at her. 'I thought you'd enjoy it. We haven't been out together much. I wanted to take you somewhere nice, perhaps go shopping later.'

'We shan't have much time for shopping.' Sara turned her head as she spoke. 'Ring your friend back, Richard.' She stopped as Richard caught her shoulders and turned her to face him.

'What is all this?' he asked, his eyes intent. 'When I say I want to be with you, I mean it. Why are you so edgy? Stop expecting every man you know to let you down, Sara.'

'We hardly know—'

Sara got no further. Richard reached out for her, pulling her hard against him and kissing her with such passion that she was shocked. Her body went limp as she felt the longing surge through her and she clung to him, wanting this to go on and on. When he released her at last, she was breathless and so was he.

'We don't know each other yet,' Richard said. 'Mainly because you've kept me at arm's length for ages—but I thought we were over all that? I thought you'd decided I could be trusted?'

'I have,' Sara said hoarsely. 'I do trust you…'

And yet there was still that little doubt in her mind. Peter had loved her mother once, but he hadn't been around when she'd really needed him. Despite his explanations and excuses, that still left a lingering doubt in Sara's mind.

'What's wrong, then?' Richard frowned. 'Is it that you have a fear of sex? Are you worried I might get impatient and force you into something you aren't ready for?'

'No…though someone did try that once. But I don't think that of you. It's just that…' Her cheeks were hot as she gazed up into his questing eyes. 'I am ready… It's just that I'm afraid. Afraid that it won't last, I suppose. Afraid of getting hurt.'

There, it was out at last. She had never admitted it even to herself before.

Richard switched off the griddle pan. 'They won't hurt for a while,' he said, taking her hand to lead her through into the sitting room. 'Sit down, Sara. We obviously need to talk.'

'I'd rather you kissed me,' Sara said as she pulled against his grasp in the hall. 'Let's go upstairs, Richard. Talking isn't going to stop me being afraid of being let down, but making love will get one thing straight between us.'

'Are you sure that's what you want?' He looked puzzled. 'If you're not sure enough of me to understand that whatever I do will include you, Sara…'

She smiled and reached up to kiss him. 'I've been hurt, Richard. Only one of them tried to rape me, but there have been others who let me down. None of them really mattered, but it all mounted up in my mind, making me feel that loving someone was a fool's game. Then, when my mother died, calling for a man who never came…' Sara gave a little sob. 'That sort of thing takes a little while to get over. I loved Peter, too, and I felt he had let us both down.'

'You've had a pretty rough time.' Richard bent his head to kiss her tenderly on the mouth. 'I do care for you, Sara. You must know that.' She nodded. 'But I can't promise I won't ever hurt you. People do things without meaning to…'

She touched her forefinger to his lips. 'Take me upstairs,' she whispered. 'Make love to me, Richard.'

'I've dreamed of you like this so many times,' Richard said as they lay side by side on the bed, their bodies naked, their clothes discarded on the carpet. 'You're so lovely, Sara.' He stroked the side of her cheek gently. 'Are you ready to let me love you?'

Sara nodded wordlessly. This was the moment she would normally be backing away, even if she had managed to get this far, but the shiver that went through her wasn't one of revulsion or fear. Far from it! She was eager and willing, her flesh tingling as she moved closer, pressing herself against him, trembling with pleasure as she felt the smooth, hard heat of him.

'Yes, please,' she whispered. 'I was afraid at first, but I'm not now. I want you so much, Richard…'

Her words were lost as his arms went round her, his mouth taking possession of hers in a hungry, demanding kiss that seemed to draw her into him, to make her a part of him. His hands were moving slowly, sensually down the slender length of her back, sending shivers of pleasure through her whole body. She moaned softly as he bent his head, taking her rosy nipple into his mouth, sucking and nibbling gently at her until she cried out.

His lips, tongue and hands explored every quivering inch of her soft flesh, bringing sensations that she'd never experienced before, filling her with anticipation and sensual delight. She arched her back, opening to him as his body covered hers, his masculine hardness sliding into the silky sheath of her feminine warmth. He moved with a slow deliberation that made her gasp and writhe beneath him, their passion mounting little by little until it suddenly exploded into sheer delight.

Afterwards, they lay entwined, bodies slippery with perspiration, eyes closed, hearts beating close, minds attuned. There was no need for words. Sara felt wonderful…free. It was as if a shadow had somehow been lifted from her. She wanted to laugh, to cry, to sing…to dance. If this was what it felt like to be in love, then she'd never felt it before—and it was good.

'Happier now?' Richard asked at last, his hand idly stroking her thigh. He bent over her, gazing down at her face as she sighed. 'It was good between us, wasn't it? You're not afraid I'll just disappear without telling you now?'

'No…' She gave a gurgle of happiness. 'No, I don't think you'll do that, Richard. Whatever this is between us, it is too important to us both, isn't it?'

'Yes, my darling.' He bent and kissed her nose. 'Now, I'm going to take a shower, then rescue our lunch. I'm starving.'

Sara nodded dreamily. She watched as he walked through to the bathroom. He hadn't bothered to put his clothes on and she was at liberty to take note of the fact that he had a fabulous body.

She lay content until he came back and began to dress, then went through to take a quick shower herself. When she got down to the kitchen, Richard was dishing up the salad.

'I hope you like your steak well done,' he said with a grimace. 'I had to warm it through again.'

'I doubt I shall taste it,' Sara said, giving him a wicked look. 'I can still taste you.'

Richard leaned forward to kiss her on the lips. 'I like the taste of you,' he said. 'Do you have to go back to your house tonight?'

'No, I don't have to,' Sara said. 'I could ring Maureen and tell her not to worry.'

Richard nodded, looking at her thoughtfully. 'You said earlier you liked this cottage. Jonathan might sell if I asked…'

Sara's heart leapt as she saw the look in his eyes. 'I think it's beautiful, but wouldn't it be better for you to buy something closer to a mainline station?'

'Perhaps…' Richard frowned. 'I could keep it on for a while anyway, just until we know where we're going. It wouldn't be suitable for long if I take the London job.'

'If?' Sara's gaze narrowed. 'I thought that was what you wanted?'

'Yes, professionally, but if it's going to spoil things for us…'

'What's your alternative?'

'I could work for the Rosewell for more than the two days I've promised. It would mean we could have more time together.'

'No.' Sara shook her head. 'I don't want you to give up your NHS work for my sake. Let's give ourselves a little time.'

'But, in the meantime, would you consider moving in here with me?'

'I can't, Richard,' Sara said. 'I'll stay tonight—but I'd

have to give Maureen and Phyllis time to get someone else to share. They need a third tenant to pay their rent. No, let's take things easily, see whether or not you get the job in London—and then decide what to do for the best. Whatever happens, you'll have free days. I can come down to London—or you can come here. It's just a case of working out how to fit in with each other.'

'Yes,' he said, but looked doubtful. 'It's what we shall have to do for the time being—but it won't work for long, Sara. If I'm going to be living in London most of the time, you'll need to look for a job there, too.'

'Yes…' Sara looked down at her plate. 'Yes, I'll think about it.'

It wouldn't be easy, giving up her job at St Saviour's. She'd settled in well and was enjoying her work.

'We don't have to think about it now,' she said. 'Let's eat or the steak will go cold again…'

CHAPTER NINE

SARA was in the kitchen preparing breakfast the next morning when the doorbell rang. She went out into the hall to listen. Richard was still in the shower. She would have to answer it herself.

She opened the door to a tall, distinguished-looking man in his mid-fifties. He had a smile on his face, which faded as he saw her.

'I guess I must have the wrong address,' he said, his eyes going over her with displeasure. Sara was wearing Richard's dressing gown, which was obviously too large for her. 'I was looking for Richard Dalton.'

'This is the right house,' Sara said, feeling oddly afraid of this man, though she didn't know why she should. 'Richard is in the shower at the moment. I was getting breakfast. We have to leave for London in half an hour— he has an interview.'

'That's why I drove up so early, to make sure of seeing him before I leave for the States,' the man said, his eyes hard and cold. 'I don't know if he's mentioned me. I'm Kurt Stolenburg. Richard was engaged to my daughter before she died.'

The anger in the stranger's eyes chilled Sara. She knew that it had shocked him to find her here—having obviously spent the night—and he wasn't too pleased.

'No, he hasn't mentioned you,' Sara replied truthfully. 'I knew you telephoned yesterday afternoon—but I didn't know you were Beth's father.'

'Richard *has* mentioned her, then?' Kurt's eyes snapped with fury. 'I must say I'm surprised that—'

'Won't you come in?' Sara said hurriedly. 'I think anything you have to say should be said to Richard, don't you?' Her head went up proudly. 'I don't know you, Mr Stolenburg, and I didn't know Beth—but Richard is a friend.'

His mouth set in a grim line, but he didn't say anything more other than to ask if she would let Richard know he was there.

'Yes, of course,' she said. 'If you would wait in there…' She indicated the sitting room, then fled straight up the stairs.

Richard was coming out of the shower as she entered the bedroom they'd shared the previous night. 'What's wrong?'

'Your friend—Kurt Stolenburg has arrived. I just let him in,' she said, keeping her voice level with difficulty. 'Look, Richard. I'm going to get dressed and go home. Don't bother to pick me up. You'll be in too much hurry when you leave here—and I have lots to do.' She darted forward to kiss his cheek. 'Good luck with the interview. Ring me as soon as you get through—let me know what happened.'

'Yes, of course.' Richard frowned. 'What did Kurt say to upset you? I suppose I can guess.'

'He didn't say much, but he wasn't pleased to find a woman wearing your dressing-gown. I think you had better go and speak to him, Richard. I'll see myself out.'

She'd been dressing all this time. Now she picked up her bag and walked towards the door. Richard followed, catching her arm to turn her back to face him. He kissed her swiftly on the mouth.

'Don't forget last night, Sara—and don't start imagining things. Just remember the way we are together. We mean too much to each other to let something like this come between us.'

Sara's eyes were dark with hurt as she gazed up at him. 'Why didn't you tell me last night that the phone call was from Beth's father?'

'It wasn't important,' he said. 'I thought you knew. Besides, I didn't want to spoil our evening. Believe me, Sara, that's all over. All I've been feeling for a long time is the guilt. Please, believe me, Sara.'

She nodded, then pulled away from his grasp. 'Let me know how you get on,' she said, and went out the door.

She passed the sitting room without glancing in, knowing that she didn't want to face Kurt Stolenburg again. She didn't know why he'd come down here to see Richard, but she didn't want to be involved. Their relationship was still too fragile to risk it by bringing back an emotional tangle from the past.

Sara was eating grapes and yogurt as Maureen came in. Maureen frowned disapprovingly over her choice of a meal. Sara always stopped eating properly when she was upset, though at other times she ate like a horse!

'Where did you come from?' Maureen asked. 'I thought you were going to London with Richard today?'

'Yes, I was,' Sara said, and sighed. 'But an unexpected arrival changed my plans.'

'What do you mean?' Maureen frowned. Sara was looking unhappy. 'Not a woman from the past?'

'It concerns a woman,' Sara said, screwing up her face. 'A woman who died. I can't tell you more than that, Maureen. It isn't my secret to tell—but I'll tell you this much—it's harder to fight a ghost than a living rival.'

'I always thought there was something about him,'

Maureen said, looking thoughtful. 'It's in his eyes…suffering.' Her gaze narrowed intently. 'That doesn't explain why you're here moping, though. You should have stood up to whatever it was—gone with him. Fought for him. You're a fool if you let an old love affair spoil your life, Sara.'

Sara nodded. 'Yes, I know. I left on impulse,' she said. 'I suppose I should have stayed and given Richard moral support—but I felt very much in the way. Beth's father drove up from London in the early hours to speak to Richard. I don't know why…'

'You think he wants him to go back to America?' Maureen nodded, understanding Sara's mood now. 'And you think if he goes that will be that?'

'Kurt Stolenburg resented my being there,' Sara said. 'Richard was engaged to his daughter. We hardly know one another. If he's in America and I'm here, I just don't stand a chance against his memories.'

'She's dead, for goodness' sake!' Maureen looked angry. 'He can't think he has a right to dictate what Richard does for—' She broke off as the doorbell rang. 'I'll go…'

'No, let me,' Sara said. 'I've got a feeling it might be for me.'

She was trembling inside as she went to answer the door, and wasn't surprised as she opened it to discover Kurt Stolenburg standing on her step.

'Miss Sara Linden?' His smile was forced and unpleasant. 'Richard told me where I could find you. Would it be asking too much if I requested five minutes of your time?'

'I don't think we can have much to say to each other, sir.'

'On the contrary, I believe we have a great deal. Please, may I come in?'

Sara stood back reluctantly to admit him. Maureen had parked herself on the sofa, and by the look on her face nothing less than a ten ton lorry was going to shift her.

'Please, sit down,' Sara said. 'May I get you some coffee?'

'No, thank you. I won't sit,' Kurt said, his eyes cold, angry. 'I've come here to tell you some things you ought to know about Richard Dalton.'

'You can have nothing to tell me that I want to know.'

'My daughter would still be alive if it were not for that man. She died horribly, Miss Linden—and it was Richard's fault.'

'What do you mean?' Sara felt a cold trickle run down her spine. Was there more to this than Richard had told her? 'What did Richard do that was so very terrible?'

'He was engaged to my daughter but he let her down. He made Beth very unhappy.'

'Because he refused to do another operation? Surely if that was his professional opinion...'

'That was only a part of it,' the enraged father said. 'She believed he was seeing another woman...and that broke her heart. He'd promised to marry her, but he was carrying on a secret affair.'

'No, he couldn't have been...'

Sara felt the pain strike at her heart. It was the one thing she couldn't condone. Richard had done to Beth what she'd believed Peter Myers had done to her mother!

'I tried to tell her she was wrong,' Kurt went on, a gleam in his eyes as if he knew he'd struck home. 'But she knew, Miss Linden—a woman always does in her heart.'

The words Sara's own mother had used when she'd lain dying!

Sara gave a whimper of pain and turned away, clutching at herself. If Richard could do that to the girl he was engaged to, then he wasn't the man she'd believed him to be. He wasn't to be trusted, wasn't to be loved—but she already loved him.

'He's lying,' Maureen said. 'Don't believe him, Sara. He wants you to believe him so that you break it off with Richard. He's out for revenge.'

Sara nodded, took a deep breath and turned back to Kurt. This was a vicious attempt to hurt her and spoil things for Richard. The man was obviously obsessed by his anger and hatred of Richard.

'Maureen is right,' she said. 'I'm afraid your little ruse has failed, Mr Stolenburg. I don't believe you. I think you made this story up to cause a split between Richard and me.'

'You think so?' He took a brown envelope out of his overcoat pocket. 'I paid for an investigation, hoping to set my daughter's mind at rest, Miss Linden—that's what they came up with. Photographs don't lie. I have another set. You can keep these.' He offered the envelope and when she refused to take it he laid it on the sideboard. 'He's responsible for Beth's death. He let her down and he will let you down. Men like him never stay faithful for long.'

Sara raised her head. 'I would be grateful if you would leave now,' she said. 'And take your pictures with you. I have no interest in your dirty little schemes.'

Kurt Stolenburg glared at her. 'You'll change your tune when he does the same to you as he did to my Beth,' he said bitterly.

'Please, leave—or I shall ring the police,' Sara said, but she was trembling.

'Get the hell out of here.' Maureen stood up and put her arm about Sara. 'You're a bully and a liar, Mr

Stolenburg—and you can take this filth with you!' She had picked up the envelope and now threw it at him. It hit him in the face and then fell to the ground.

He left it lying there, then turned and walked out, slamming the door shut behind him.

Maureen picked the envelope up, her intention obviously to follow and thrust it at him.

'No,' Sara said. 'Keep it. I'll give it to Richard. I think he should know what his so-called friend has done.'

'You're not going to look at it, are you?'

Sara shook her head. 'No. I don't want to see it, whatever it is. I shall simply return it to Richard.'

Maureen looked at her oddly. 'You don't believe that brute—do you?'

'I'm not sure,' Sara said, tears stinging her eyes. She refused to let them fall even though she was utterly miserable. 'I don't want to believe it, Maureen, but I know Richard feels very guilty over Beth's death. It's possible that Mr Stolenburg was telling the truth. I know he wanted me to break it off with Richard, but it might be true that…' She broke off, unable to go on.

'I don't believe it,' Maureen said staunchly. 'Not for one minute—not Richard. He's just not the type to let a woman he cared for down. Your stepfather—yes, I'll believe it of him. Maybe in his case it was weakness, because he couldn't stand to see your mother so ill, but Richard isn't weak. If he was having an affair—which I doubt—he had good reason for it. Maybe she let him down first…'

'That was Peter's excuse,' Sara said in a voice that reflected her pain. 'He said my mother had an affair some years before she died. They made it up, but then he met someone he liked and…he swore he never meant to hurt Mum, but he did, even if he wasn't actually having an affair. Not meaning to do something doesn't excuse what he did—and it doesn't excuse Richard if he did the same. He knew Beth was vulnerable. At the very least he should have been honest with her—broken off their engagement.'

'Well, I would think long and hard before you take Mr Stolenburg's word,' Maureen said. 'You've been offered a chance of happiness, Sara. You would be a fool to let something like this stand in your way. In my opinion, Richard is worth fighting for.'

Richard left the interview feeling pleased. He hadn't been offered the job on the spot, because there were other applicants, but he had good reason to feel encouraged. The panel had consisted of three men and two women, all of them highly experienced medical personnel, and they'd asked a lot of very intelligent questions.

One woman had been concerned about the break in his surgical career, but when he told her it had been due to a bereavement she'd appeared to accept his statement.

He'd been told that he would hear within a week and asked when he could begin if selected.

'About mid-March,' Richard had told them.

He'd booked out the first two weeks of the month to follow up his commitment to Chris, knowing that the first of the operations would be the most difficult. He would have Chris in early, talk him through what he was going to do and give him careful counselling.

He anticipated it would take him several hours to rebuild the smashed cheekbone, using bone taken from Chris's thigh. Subsequent operations would be to put right as much as possible of the scarring, but they wouldn't need to be done immediately, and could be fitted in as and when he had an opening in his schedule.

If this job came off, it would be an extremely busy schedule. He frowned as he thought about the best way to sort out his accommodation problems. Now that the sale of his New York apartment was going through, he would have money to play with. He could afford to buy an apartment in London, where he could spend part of the week, and the cottage Sara liked so much—providing Jon was prepared to sell, of course.

Unless he bought a larger house with a garden somewhere like Hampstead? Richard thought his own preference might be for something like that…but he was jumping the gun. He hadn't actually been offered the position yet, and after the way Sara had reacted this morning, his private life was once again at risk.

He cursed Kurt for whatever he had said to her. It must have been something pretty unpleasant to make her run off like that. Kurt had asked where he could find Sara—wanting to apologize for scaring her off, he'd said—but Richard had refused to give him her address.

Kurt blamed Richard for Beth's death. He'd accused Richard of making Beth's life intolerable, of driving her to suicide, his manner that of a man who was demented by his grief. Richard had blamed himself, but in his heart he knew he wasn't to blame. He'd done nothing to harm her…except that she'd sensed he hadn't been in love with her. He'd proposed one day after he'd found her weeping in her father's garden, his sympathy aroused by her extreme vulnerability. A vulnerability which he believed had been due as much to her domineering father as anything else.

It had been the biggest mistake of his life. He'd been fond of Beth—but he hadn't been in love with her. Had they married, he might, without meaning to, quite possibly have made her very unhappy.

He had certainly not done anything to deserve the abuse Kurt had flung at him. It had been unexpected, because they had always been friends until then. But Kurt had had some ridiculous notion that Richard had been cheating on Beth.

Richard frowned as he recalled the night when Beth's best friend had draped herself all over him at a party. Some photographer had taken pictures when Karen had been kissing nim. Goodness knew, he hadn't encouraged her, but he'd found Beth in floods of tears later that evening. It was then she'd begged him to make her scars go away—and he'd told her he hadn't thought it was necessary.

Richard so often wished he could go back to that night. He'd never meant to hurt Beth. But how could he have known she'd been so miserable she would take her own life?

If she'd been jealous of Karen, she'd been wrong to be. He hadn't even liked the woman, and he certainly hadn't wanted to make love to her. The possibility of having an affair with her had never entered his head—to be accused of it by Kurt had not only been unfair but also ridiculous.

Richard tried telephoning Sara a couple of times on the train going home, but all he got was the answering machine. He frowned, wondering where she was. As far as he knew, she didn't have to start at St Saviour's until half past seven. He'd hoped to reach her, tell her his news, and was frustrated by his inability to get past that damned machine.

He'd planned something special for this London trip and he was annoyed that Kurt's uninvited arrival which seemed to have little purpose beyond stirring up the bad feeling between them, had spoiled everything.

When Richard arrived at the station, he got into his car to begin the forty-five-minute drive back to the village. It would be a tiring journey if he had to do it regularly. If Sara really wanted to live in this area, he might have to look for a nice cottage nearer King's Lynn, but it would be much better if she could be persuaded to look for a job in London so that they could be together more often. They were both devoted to their work, but they needed a private life, too.

He was thoughtful as he at last drew up outside Sara's home. It was half past six. They would manage perhaps half an hour together before they both had to work—but that was better than nothing. They had a lot to discuss.

Sara was coming out of the house as he drew into the kerb. She stopped as she saw him, looking indecisive, then went back to the front door and waited.

'I wasn't sure if you would get back...'

'I tried to ring several times, but I could only get the machine.'

'Oh, sorry. I didn't realize we'd turned the ringer off the phone.' Sara did that sometimes when she needed to sleep through the day.

'It was frustrating trying to get through. I wanted to tell you my news.'

'Yes, of course...' Sara led the way inside the cottage. She looked at him hesitantly. 'How did it go?'

'Quite well, I think. One woman was uncertain about me—but I think the others liked me.'

Sara nodded. 'I had a visitor this morning—Kurt Stolenburg. He said you gave him my address.'

'I did no such thing. He asked and I refused,' Richard said angrily. 'He must have taken it from my address book, which was on the hall table, when he went to the cloakroom.' He frowned, looking at her thoughtfully. 'What did he say to you?'

Sara picked up the large envelope and handed it to him. 'I haven't looked inside, Richard, and I don't intend to—but he said it was proof that you were cheating on Beth, that it was your affair that led her to kill herself, not the scars you refused to operate on.'

'Why are you giving it to me?'

'I thought you should have it,' Sara replied, her face pale and strained. 'I thought you should know what he was saying about you. He obviously hates you, Richard. He may try to harm you in some way.'

'He can do his damnedest!' Richard said hoarsely. 'I know what's in here, Sara. The pictures were taken at a party—they are of Beth's best friend. She kissed me. It was entirely her idea. I think she may have been drunk—'

'I don't need to know,' Sara said stiffly. 'Whatever happened is your affair, Richard. Between you and Beth.'

'But you do believe I cheated on her, don't you?'

Sara hesitated, then raised her eyes to his. 'I don't want to believe it, Richard. I—I don't know…'

Richard felt the anger flare inside him. How could she doubt him after the previous night? How could she think he would cheat on the lovely, vulnerable girl who had been his fiancée? He might have realised he'd not been in love with Beth, but he'd cared about her—and had felt a terrible agony when she'd died. His guilt had stayed with him for months, but he hadn't been guilty of betraying Beth by having an affair.

'I told you I felt guilty for having neglected her, but that's all there was to it.'

'I know. I'm sorry. It's just that…'

'Just nothing!' Richard said furiously. 'If you can believe that of me, there's nothing left to say. Without trust, love isn't worth having. Believe me, I know! I've been through this once before, and I certainly don't need it from you!'

'Richard…' The cry was from Sara's heart, stopping him in his tracks as he was about to storm off. 'I'm sorry.'

'So am I,' he said, and his face was an iron mask. 'I'm going away for a few days. I need to think about this, Sara. And you should think seriously about what kind of a future you want. I'll be in touch, but not for a while.'

'Where are you going?' Her heart jerked painfully. She wanted to beg him not to leave, but the words wouldn't come.

'To the Rosewell,' Richard said. 'I've arranged to do an operation for the clinic to make up for the time I'll be taking off next month to do Chris's restructure.'

Sara gulped, the tears beginning to slip down her cheeks as Richard walked out to his car, got in and drove off without looking at her.

What a fool she'd been to let Kurt Stolenburg's poisonous words get to her. He'd wanted to make trouble for Richard, to spoil his life. Now he had exactly what he wanted…

'I'm glad to see you back,' Gillian said when Sara went onto the wards that evening. 'Have you heard the latest?'

'What do you mean?' Sara pulled her wandering thoughts back to the present. She was at work now and her personal problems had to be stored away for the next few hours. There was always a certain amount of gossip going the rounds. 'What happened while I was away?'

'They're talking about closing two of our wards—the hospital is way over budget again this quarter. They need money to set up the new surgical unit—apparently, that has priority.'

'You mean the G wards?' Sara was shocked by the news. 'But they can't! If they closed two of our wards...' She was too distressed by the prospect to continue.

'Exactly!' Gillian said dourly. 'It will mean we shan't get to work together. One of us will probably have to move onto Surgical. They're always needing more nurses there.'

'What about the patients?' Sara wanted to know. 'St Saviour's has always been known for the quality of its care. This means we'll have to have a much faster turn-around on G wards, which means patients will have to be moved. Either to a nursing home or a hospice.'

'It won't be the same,' Gillian said. 'We always had time to get to know everyone. We shan't in future.'

Sara nodded. She was thoughtful as she made her first round of the evening. What would happen to people like Mrs Rowe? She'd been brought in with a broken hip. It was mending well, but she was still far too fragile to be sent home. Another two weeks and she might be able to cope, provided she was given all the attention and phys-iotherapy she needed. She would get that at St Saviour's, but if she was passed on too soon to a residential home for old people...even a nursing home would be unlikely to offer as efficient a service as they'd prided themselves on giving here.

And it was all due to a lack of money in the funding system. Sara was aware of feeling angry. She wasn't sure she would want to go on working here if her wards were closed.

*   *   *

Maureen was in when Sara got home the next morning. She was cooking sausages, bacon, mushrooms and tomatoes.

'There's plenty for you,' she said. 'I felt like getting a proper meal, and I'll bet you haven't eaten much.'

'No, I haven't had time,' Sara replied. 'We had three emergency admissions last night. One of them died.'

'That's pretty rotten,' Maureen said sympathetically. 'Got you down, has it?'

'It's not just that…'

Sara explained about the closure of the wards. Maureen nodded as she carried two plates of piping hot food to the table.

'I did hear it was on the cards. What will you do if they go ahead?'

'I'm not sure.' Sara glanced towards the answering machine. 'Any messages?'

'None, I'm afraid.'

'I thought Peter might have rung. He wants to discuss selling the house. He says he doesn't want to live there any longer. And he feels that I ought to have been left a share—so he's proposing to give me half of the money. I told him it doesn't matter to me any more. I was angry with him because I thought he'd let Mum and me down, but now I'm over all that—but he's insisting on giving me half the proceeds.'

'Don't knock it,' Maureen replied with a grin. 'Never say no when someone wants to give you money, love. It comes in mighty handy when you're old and grey—the way I soon shall be.'

They both laughed together.

'About the ward closures—didn't you say Richard might be going to work in London?' Maureen asked. Sara nodded, her gaze dropping as she saw the look in her friend's eyes. 'Why don't you start looking for a job in that direction? It would be better for you both.'

'I could…' Sara said. 'But I'm not even sure I shall be seeing Richard again. He said he would be in touch, but not for a while.'

It was really Richard she'd been expecting a call from. She'd hoped he would relent and ring her, but it seemed he was disgusted with her—and in her heart she couldn't blame him.

She didn't feel like eating the breakfast her friend had prepared, but couldn't offend her by refusing. Afterwards, she did the washing up, then went upstairs to shower, before tumbling into bed.

That's when the wanting and the hurting really began to bite. It was impossible not to remember the feel of Richard's smooth skin close to hers, the smell and taste of him. She'd managed to block him out completely while she'd been working. As always, her patients came first when she was on the wards, but now her whole body seemed to throb with the need Richard's loving had aroused in her.

She wanted to be with him, in his arms. What an idiot she'd been to doubt Richard even for a few minutes. Kurt Stolenburg's bitter words had been meant to hurt her. Maureen had warned her not to listen, but she hadn't been able to prevent the doubts creeping in—and Richard had sensed them.

It was time she let go of the past. Sara faced the truth. Her mother had been desperately ill. It was often the case that people who were that ill let things play on their minds. Sara's mother had believed her husband had been betraying her, but Peter had merely been weak. He hadn't visited the hospital as often as he should have done, but that had been because he hadn't been able to face his wife's illness, not because he hadn't cared.

Because Peter had been weak, it didn't mean that Sara was right to distrust every man. Richard was strong, much stronger than her stepfather, but he was also gentle, kind and caring. From the very beginning he'd been there for her, saving her from being abused by a drunken bully, helping her when she'd come off her cousin's bike— helping Chris.

He was definitely a white knight, she thought. Or a knight in a white coat... A mental picture of Richard charging to the rescue in his surgical gear, scalpel in hand, made her laugh. He was dedicated to his work— was it likely that such a man would have an affair when he was engaged to a girl he thought of as vulnerable?

Of course not! Sara should have known. Richard had every right to feel angry with her. For her to have doubted him after all they'd been to each other was especially hurtful.

She knew she ought to apologize. She would do so as soon as she got the chance—but was it too late?

Richard had said he needed time to think. Supposing he decided he couldn't be bothered with a woman who made love with him one minute, then listened to the spiteful words of a bitter man the next?

CHAPTER TEN

RICHARD looked round at his assembled team. He'd talked to them individually the previous day and was satisfied that they all knew what was expected of them. It was, by his standards, a simple procedure that morning. The patient was in her mid-forties, in good health and had just been divorced. She needed the confidence a sub-periostial face lift would give her.

Richard had talked to her on two separate occasions. She had spoken to her own doctor about the procedure several times, and had been to the clinic to have consultations with a skin specialist.

Richard had sat on the edge of her bed the previous evening and gone through everything again, making sure she understood.

'You do understand that a face-lift can't stop the ageing process, but will simply reduce some visible aspects?'

'Yes.' She smiled at him hopefully. 'I just need to look a little less wrinkled. I want to work as a PR consultant, and this will give me more confidence.'

'And you've read all the literature? You understand there could be some loss of feeling in the cheeks and ears, and very occasionally motor nerves around the mouth and eyebrows may be affected?'

'Yes. I've assessed the risks. I still want to go ahead, that's why I'm here.'

'It is my duty to warn you,' Richard said, and smiled at her reassuringly. 'But I've had many more complicated cases than yours, Marie, and very few have ever resulted in serious problems for the patient—that's more likely in trauma cases, where the damage is already done and we have to repair it as best we can. Apart from some initial swelling and pain, you'll be fine.'

'I have perfect confidence in you, Mr Dalton. You were highly recommended.'

Marie was sedated and ready. Richard had wondered whether he might find it difficult to recapture his old skill and confidence. Now that he was in Theatre, his team alert and expectant, the adrenaline flowed and he felt the thrill his work had always given him. A plastic surgeon needed to be versatile and inventive. He also needed steady hands and nerves of steel.

The lamp he wore strapped to his head provided focused illumination over the specific areas he would be working on. The technique he was using was an endoscopic lift, or keyhole surgery. The skin would be lifted off the bone and the muscles weakened using an endoscopic camera with fibre-optic lights. That would enable Richard to ease the frown lines, and mouth to nose lines, a technique more often used on younger patients. The procedure was for two incisions to be made in the skin, then the endoscope and instruments were fed through and the underlying periosteum pulled up the face. Once this procedure was complete, he would do a little eyelid-tightening.

Richard smiled at his team.

'I think Marie is well away now. Shall we begin?'

He made the first incisions through the skin of Marie's face, then the drug clonidine was administered to lower blood pressure and reduce pain, a local anaesthetic for post-operative recovery, and adrenaline to control the bleeding to allow for accuracy of surgery.

Richard began with the brow lift, a procedure that

would take forty-five minutes. He was focused, his mind
totally on the job in hand.

Richard had begun surgery at 9.15. He left Theatre at
12.05, feeling a sense of huge satisfaction. The work had
gone perfectly, with no complications. He was quite certain that when Marie's face was completely healed,
which might take several weeks, she would be thrilled
with her new look.

'Oh, Mr Dalton.' The receptionist caught up with him.
'There was a telephone call for you while you were in
surgery: Sister Linden. She asked if you would call back
when you were free.'

'Thank you.'

Richard nodded his thanks but carried on to the staff
canteen, where he ordered fresh salmon and salad sand-
wiches and a mineral water. He frowned as he ate his
solitary meal. It had been almost two weeks now since
he'd spoken to Sara. He ought to have called her before
this, but he'd been busy seeing potential patients and getting to know his colleagues both at the Rosewell and in
London.

The NHS position had been offered within two days
of his interview. The chairman of the panel had called
him personally to tell him how eager they were to have
him on board.

He had accepted and was now negotiating the lease of
a small flat near the hospital. Since he had no idea where
his private life was heading, he'd decided to rent for the
time being. At the moment he was staying in staff accommodation at the Rosewell. He was due to operate on
Chris the next day, and he would leave to take up his
post in London the following day, after checking on both
his patients.

He would be working on a Monday, Tuesday and Wednesday in London, then Friday and Saturday at the Rosewell. It was an arrangement that left him two free days a week, though he would have to use a part of them for travelling. It would, however, ensure that he had some free time—and also allowed for him to be called in for emergencies, which were more likely to be in London than at the clinic. His appointments at the Rosewell were more straightforward, scheduled weeks or months ahead to allow his patients to rearrange their own lives.

What was he going to do about Sara? Richard had been very angry the day they'd parted. He had left believing that she really couldn't be committed to their relationship if she was ready to accept the word of a stranger—and he'd seen the doubts in her eyes.

He'd been hurt, but also wary. Having been through the trauma of his relationship with Beth, Richard was uneasy about plunging into another. If Sara didn't trust him now, how would she feel when they were living together? Would she start accusing him of having been with other women whenever he was late home? Would she be jealous if her friends started to flirt with him?

Richard wasn't sure he could take all that again. At first he'd thought it might be best to end their affair swiftly—a quick, clean cut with the minimum amount of pain for them both. Yet he hadn't been able to forget her—the taste and scent of her, the sweetness of their loving. Perhaps he was misjudging her? Beth had been a vulnerable girl, but Sara was a woman and far more mature.

He'd hesitated about phoning, not even sure if she wanted to hear from him, but now she'd phoned. Should he ring back? Or perhaps it might be better to drop by on his free day, before he went down to London? Yes, he would prefer that. It would be better if they met face to face.

It had cost Sara's pride to ring and leave a message at the Rosewell. She'd waited for Richard to telephone her, but it seemed he had no intention of doing so, and Sara was becoming desperate. She couldn't let him walk out of her life without at least trying to heal the breach between them—but she'd made the effort in vain. Richard hadn't returned her call.

She came out of the shower that morning, towelling herself as she wondered what to do now. Chris was having his operation that day so there was no point in ringing again. Richard would be tied up in surgery for hours.

She was anxious about her cousin, knowing that however good the surgical team there was always a risk of complications. Her aunt was staying at the Rosewell for a couple of days and would let her know when Chris was out of Theatre.

Sara absent-mindedly made a routine examination of her breasts. She did it every few weeks, usually when she had bathed, thinking of it as a safety net. It was only sensible when there was a history of breast cancer in her family. Her fingers moved over the familiar area and then back again. She frowned as she felt some definite changes, a little lumpiness that hadn't been there the last time she'd checked. Now that she thought about it, her breasts felt different, more tender than usual.

A thought flashed into her mind, but she dismissed it almost at once. She couldn't be pregnant!

Dismissing the nagging worry from her mind, Sara dressed and left the house. She got into her car and drove down to the village. She had the day off, and it was her turn to shop.

In the shop she bumped into Mrs Reed, the lady who'd had so much trouble with her insulin injections. She pounced on Sara with evident delight.

'Oh, I was hoping to see you,' she said. 'I wanted to tell you how much better I feel. That marvellous contraption you got for me is so easy to use and I'm getting on so well. I wanted to say thank you for taking so much time and trouble to help me, Sister Linden. I'm so much better that I'm going on holiday with my friend very soon. We're off to Spain!'

'Well, that's wonderful news. I'm so pleased for you.'

'I might even find myself a new man,' Mrs Reed told her. 'I'm a new woman—so why shouldn't I find a new man?'

Sara chuckled as the elderly lady left the shop with her purchases. Who said nursing on geriatric wards was depressing? Sometimes nursing could be very rewarding!

It was as she'd just left the store with her loaded trolley, which she parked at the back of her car and proceeded to unload, that she heard her name called. Turning, she found herself being hailed by Angela Harper. Richard's sister! She felt guilty as Angela came hurrying up to her. She hadn't been near for ages, partly because she wasn't sure whether Richard had mentioned her to Angela or not.

'I'm glad I caught you,' Angela said, coming to kiss her cheek. 'I've been meaning to telephone. I'm giving a little party this weekend. Would you like to come?'

'I'm not sure. I'm working on Saturday evening...'

'It's Sunday afternoon actually, so that Richard can come along,' Angela said. 'You know he starts his new job in London next Monday?' Sara shook her head, and Angela frowned. 'I was sure he would have told you...

Jack thought…' She blushed. 'Well, he said he thought you two might be getting friendly.'

'We are…were…' Sara swallowed hard, not wanting Richard's sister to guess how painful this conversation was for her. 'We had a bit of a misunderstanding over something. I've been waiting for Richard to ring.'

'And he hasn't?' Angela shook her head. 'Typical of my brother! We didn't hear from him for months after he went off to Africa, then one day he just turned up out of the blue and said he wanted to see his family. Had no idea that we'd all been worried over him.' She frowned. 'My family are all he has, of course. Our parents died when we were just kids. I do worry about him, Sara. I was hoping he was going to settle down at last.'

'Maybe he will…' Sara lifted her chin, letting pride carry her through. 'Look, I have to go now, Angela—but I will come on Sunday.'

'Oh, I'm so glad,' Angela said. 'Once you and Richard get together, you can probably sort it out—whatever it is.'

'Yes, perhaps.' Sara smiled bravely. 'What time?'

'About three,' Angela said. 'Take care of yourself, love—you're looking a bit peaky.'

Sara smiled again and shook her head, but she was thoughtful as she got into the car. Now she thought about it, she wasn't feeling exactly A1. She had put it down to not sleeping well, but there was that change to her breasts. She might be wise to book an appointment with her own doctor.

'Chris is out of surgery,' Aunt Mary said when she rang just before Sara left for work that evening. 'I spoke to Richard afterwards and he said the operation had gone well. Chris is going to look almost like his old self, Sara, though he may have some superficial scarring. But what does that matter? Besides, Richard has promised to do another operation if he needs it.'

'That was good of him,' Sara said. 'I'm really pleased Chris is OK.'

'You sound a little odd,' her aunt said. 'Is anything the matter?'

'I'm just a little tired.'

'Have you been eating properly? You work too hard, Sara.'

'Yes, perhaps. I don't think I can get down to the Rosewell to see Chris. Give him my love and tell him I'll come over when he's home.'

'Yes, of course—and take care of yourself, love.'

Sara replaced the receiver. She was definitely feeling tired and not like herself. Perhaps it was her diet. She would have to try and eat a little more starch and protein—especially if her suspicions were correct. She would be eating for two then and not just for one.

She had booked an appointment with her doctor, but it was impossible to get in for some little time ahead. Her tiredness and the changes to her breasts might be due to pre-menstrual fluctuations… Sara frowned as she tried to recall when she'd had her last period. Was she about due…or was she a few days overdue?

She couldn't remember. Because she hadn't been in a sexual relationship for such a long time, she hadn't bothered to keep a check…neither had she taken any precautions. She just hadn't thought about it that night, had been carried away by her emotional needs and desires.

Sara frowned. What was she going to do if she was carrying Richard's child? How would he feel about things? Neither of them had been thinking responsibly that night… Would he want her to keep it or have an abortion?

If she had his child, it would present all sorts of problems with her career. She had been thinking of leaving St Saviour's, but even though she knew it would be discriminatory to be denied a job because she would be needing maternity leave, anyone might think twice about taking her on.

But she didn't know for certain yet! Nor did she know what her meeting with Richard on Sunday would bring forth.

Sara showered and dressed in casual trousers and a sloppy cotton shirt on Sunday morning. She was just going to laze around for most of the morning, eat a cheese and salad sandwich for lunch, then get ready for Angela's party.

Phyllis was coming out of the kitchen as she went downstairs. Her face was white and it was clear she was under a terrific strain.

'What's wrong?' Sara asked. She wasn't quite as close to Phyllis as to Maureen, but they were friends and she sensed something was up. 'You look terrible.'

'I've got pain in my side,' Phyllis said, and gasped in agony. 'I think it must be appendicitis, Sara.' She bit down on her lip and doubled over as the pain caught her off balance and she almost fell. Sara went to her at once, supporting her to the sofa. 'I think…I think I need a doctor.'

'Sit there and get your breath, love. I'll call an ambulance.'

Phyllis was gasping as the pain doubled her up once more.

Sara was already halfway to the phone. She dialled the

emergency number, feeling anxious. Phyllis's colour was bad. This looked serious. If it was appendicitis then the appendix had probably burst.

'We need an ambulance,' she told the operator. 'It's vital that it gets here as quickly as possible. I think my friend is going to need immediate surgery.'

Phyllis was sitting on the edge of the sofa. Beads of sweat stood out on her brow and she was shaking. She looked at Sara as she came back to her, fear in her eyes.

'I'm pregnant, Sara. I thought it might be appendicitis, but I've just thought…it might be something else.'

'Ectopic—an extrauterine pregnancy,' Sara said, understanding at once why the idea frightened Phyllis. It frightened her, too, for her friend's sake, but she knew she had to keep calm, to give Phyllis the reassurance she needed. 'How long is it?'

'About six weeks…' Phyllis gasped again. 'I've thought something wasn't quite right, but I didn't want to admit it. Oh, Sara, what am I going to do? I wanted this baby. Sam was going to get somewhere for us to live…so that we could be together, as a family.'

'Never mind that just now, love,' Sara said, sitting next to her to hold her hand. She had her professional cap on now. 'What we have to think about is you.'

This was a serious condition. It meant that the fertilized ovum had failed to reach the uterus and had become implanted elsewhere, probably in the uterine tube but possibly in the peritoneal cavity. At about six weeks the tube could burst, causing severe pain, shock and intra-abdominal haemorrhage. It was serious but could be treated if caught in time.

'How long have you been having the pain?'

'It started early this morning, just after I came home from my shift. I had been doing some heavy lifting and thought it was just strain…but it has been getting worse all the time.'

Sara squeezed her hand. Her throat was tight with emotion but she fought it back. It would be useless to offer her friend false hope. There was no chance of saving the baby, and they both knew it, but at least they might be in time for Phyllis.

'Hang on in there, love,' she said. 'The ambulance is on its way. Once the paramedics get here they'll be able to help with the pain.'

Phyllis looked at her, her eyes dark with fear. 'You will come with me, won't you? Please, Sara. I need you. Sam is working away this weekend. He couldn't get back in time. Stay with me…'

'Yes, of course I will. I wouldn't dream of leaving you at a time like this. It's going to be all right, love. I'll ring Sam and let him know what's happened. I'm sure he'll come as soon as he can.'

She ought to ring Angela, too, let her know she wouldn't be there. But there was no time, the ambulance had arrived. Sara forgot about her own situation as she rushed to the door to answer it, giving the paramedics an idea of what she thought might be happening, then she was accompanying Phyllis as the two young men carried her into the ambulance. This was a matter of life and death…

Richard glanced at his watch. It was four-thirty and there was no sign of Sara. She had obviously decided against coming—and that could only be because she knew he was going to be there. Was there any point in going round to her house? Or should he leave without seeing her? He had a long drive ahead of him, and he was operating in the morning.

'Stay for a bit longer,' Angela said persuasively. 'You haven't even seen Jack yet. He won't want to miss—' She broke off as her husband's key turned in the lock. 'Here he is now.'

Jack had been called out to an emergency just after lunch. He came in, kissed his wife and then looked at Richard.

'I've just heard there was an emergency call-out this morning—Sara Linden. They've taken her to St Saviour's for emergency surgery. Apparently there wasn't time to take her anywhere else. They had to call the surgeon in in a hurry.'

'Sara…an emergency operation?' Richard stared at him, feeling the shock run through him. All at once he knew that their argument didn't matter. He was in love with Sara and there was no denying it. 'What's wrong with her?'

'It came in as suspected appendicitis,' Jack said, 'but the paramedics were telling me that it might be something else…' He stopped and frowned. 'I don't know for sure, but does extrauterine pregnancy sound possible?'

'I don't know…' Richard was stunned. Such a condition wasn't likely to cause a problem after only two…nearly three weeks. If it was true it could mean that Sara had been pregnant when…but he didn't believe that! His instincts told him that she hadn't been to bed with anyone else for a long time before him. So this report was either wrong or symptoms had showed up early. Either way, it didn't matter. The important thing was what had happened to Sara. 'I'll go up straight away,' he said. 'I should think it more likely to be acute appendicitis, but I'm going to find out.'

'I told her she wasn't looking well when I saw her shopping,' Angela said. 'That's the trouble with you medical people. You're so busy looking after everyone else, you don't take care of yourselves.'

'I have to go,' Richard said, already on his way to the door. 'I'll call you later.'

He went out to his car, and was driving away when his sister came to the door. He waved, not stopping to discover whatever it was Angela wanted to tell him. At the moment all he cared about was Sara—anything else could wait!

'Sister Linden… I don't think…' The receptionist frowned as she checked her list. 'No—no, it was Staff Nurse Phyllis Jones who came in for emergency surgery. Sister Linden may have come with her. I understand they share a house in the village.'

'Staff Nurse…' Richard sagged with relief. He had been so afraid it was happening again, that he was going to lose the woman he loved. 'Thank you…thank you very much.'

He turned to leave the hospital, then stopped as he heard his name being called. He turned to see Sara coming towards him. She had obviously been crying. Her face was streaked with tears and her nose was red. Richard went to her at once, opening his arms. Sara stepped into them, and he held her, emotion washing over him in a great wave.

'Thank God!' he said. 'I thought it was you—I thought it was you, Sara.'

She gazed up at him, seeing the anguish in his face. Then she reached up to touch his cheek lovingly with her fingertips.

'It's all right, darling,' she said softly. 'I phoned Angela a few minutes ago. I'm sorry you were worried. I'm sorry I didn't ring sooner, but it was touch and go for Phyllis. I just couldn't leave until I knew she was in the clear…she came out of Theatre twenty minutes ago. I talked to the doctor, she's going to be OK. I couldn't ring before…'

'No, of course you couldn't.' Richard smiled at her. 'Angela came to the door as I was leaving, but she was too late to stop me.'

'I'm glad you came. I needed you, Richard.'

'Did you, Sara?'

'Yes. I've been needing you ever since we parted.'

He smiled, then bent his head to kiss her. 'I've been a bloody fool. What happened today has taught me that. You came in the ambulance with Phyllis?'

'Yes. She was so very upset and frightened.' She gazed at him, a teasing smile on her lips. 'Were you by any chance thinking of giving me a lift home, Richard? I was about to try and get a taxi…'

'Of course.' He pulled a rueful face. 'I'm sorry I haven't been in touch. I was coming to see you today, then Angela told me you would be at the party.'

'I intended to come,' Sara said, taking a deep breath to steady her. 'I wanted to apologize… I am sorry, Richard. I shouldn't have doubted you for a moment. Maureen was very cross with me. She said I was an idiot.'

'I must thank her for her confidence,' Richard said. He was thinking how lovely Sara looked, how much he wanted to make love to her. 'It hurt me that you could think I would be that careless of someone else's feelings.'

'Yes, but it was more than that, wasn't it?' They were outside now. It was the middle of March, the sun was bright but there was a chill wind blowing. Sara shivered, and pulled up her coat collar. 'You've been through one bad experience with a vulnerable clinging vine, haven't you? You must have wondered if you wanted to risk that again.'

Richard stood, gazing down into her face. 'I admit the thought did occur to me, Sara. Beth was so unsure of herself. She had no need to be, she was very lovely even with the scars, but she couldn't believe I loved her.'

'But you did?'

'I loved her very much as a person, as a friend. I wanted to protect her, and when I asked her to marry me I thought that meant I was in love with her. It didn't. I began to realize that after a few weeks. I loved her, but I wasn't in love—that's a very different emotion.'

'Beth knew, didn't she?'

'Yes, I'm certain she did. I believe that was why she did what she did. She must have been afraid I would break off our engagement.'

'And would you?'

'Not for the sake of anyone else. There was no other woman, Sara. It is important that you do believe that.'

'I do, Richard. I've had time to think, and I know you couldn't do something like that.'

'Good.' He nodded his satisfaction. 'At least we've made a start. I've known a lot of women, Sara. When I was a student there was a succession of temporary girl-friends. Without being vain, I must tell you that I usually have a problem fighting them off.'

'Yes, I can imagine you might.'

Sara kept her eyes lowered as they walked to his car.

'I don't try to attract them, they just come on to me—some of them quite strongly.'

'Yes, I see…' Sara waited for him to get to the point.

'So when I met a young woman who didn't want to know—' her eyes flew to his in surprise '—it came as quite a shock to my system.'

'Oh…' She felt a tingling begin at the base of her spine. 'You must have thought I was an ungracious brat.'

'No, that doesn't accurately describe my feelings,' Richard said, a smile beginning to tug at the corners of his mouth. 'Exasperation was certainly a part of it.'

'Yes, it would be. I can see that…'

Her heart was beating very fast. The look in his eyes sent shivers down her spine. He was so attractive; she couldn't help remembering the way his eyes went dark when he was making love, and the smell of his skin when it was slightly damp with sweat.

'But there was considerably more…' He pulled a wry face at her. 'Do I have to spell this out?'

'No, I don't think so,' she said, giving a gurgle of laughter. 'Maureen should be coming off shift any time now—do you still have the key to Jon's cottage, Richard?'

'I might,' he said, his eyes beginning to sparkle with a wicked delight. 'You know, I just might…'

Sara turned and half sat up, leaning over Richard to gaze down at his face. She bent to kiss him on the lips, tasting him, savouring the pleasure they had just shared.

'I missed you,' she said. 'I missed you terribly, Richard. I kept on hoping you would telephone—then, in the end, I rang the Rosewell. Did you get my message?'

'Yes.' He reached for her, pulling her down to him so that their bodies fitted together once more. 'I ought to have returned your call, but I hate deciding important things over a phone. I wanted to see you.' He grinned suddenly. 'I suppose I wanted this to happen.'

'Not as much as I did,' she said, and stroked his cheek with her fingertips. He had such strong features, and there was power in the man, the kind of shoulders you could lean on. 'I couldn't stop thinking about you and the way it is between us.'

'And I wasted all that time,' Richard said. 'I'm sorry, my darling.'

'I think it was good that you did,' Sara replied seriously. 'We both needed time to be sure of our feelings…because neither of us wants to make another mistake.'

'I know how I feel. I've known for a while.' He tipped her chin so that he could look into her eyes. 'All I need to know is whether you are ready to commit to a long-term relationship?'

'I've never felt this way about any other man,' Sara said. 'There were a few brief affairs, none of them lasted more than a few dates and some were even shorter. Except for someone in my student days…before Mum died.'

Richard nodded, looking at her with understanding. 'That really knocked you for six, didn't it?'

'Yes. It wasn't just the way she died, it was my own sense of betrayal. I had been fond of my stepfather. I felt that he'd betrayed me as much as her. I couldn't forgive him, and it made me feel no man was to be trusted. Most men I went out with wanted one thing.'

'And when they didn't get it, things went sour?' She nodded and he frowned. 'No wonder you told me you were off men. You didn't want to know me at the start—did you think I wanted my wicked way with you?'

'Oh, Richard!' Sara laughed and snuggled up to him. 'I never thought that at all. You seemed like a knight in shining armour, riding in to the rescue.'

'I'm not that,' he said, letting his fingers run through her silky hair. 'I make mistakes, Sara. When I get wrapped up in my work I can be thoughtless and distant. Do you think you can put up with that?'

'Yes, I think so.' She kissed him lightly on his naked shoulder. 'I'm a nurse, remember. I know what it's like to get wrapped up in your work, to worry about your patients even when you're supposed to be off duty.'

Richard nodded. 'We must telephone in the morning, see how Phyllis is before I leave for London.'

'Yes, we must. I feel so sorry for her. She wanted that baby.' Sara nestled against him. 'When can you come up again, Richard? Is it going to be difficult for you? Would it be easier if I came down?'

'When is your next day off?'

'If I work weekends, I can take two days off mid-week,' she said. 'Wednesday or Thursday, or both.'

'I have Thursdays free unless there's an emergency,' he said. 'If you came up on Wednesday, you could stay over and we could travel up together on Thursday afternoon.'

'That would be lovely...' She sighed with content. 'I thought it might be weeks before we got to see each other again.'

'I'll have a few hours on Thursdays and Sundays,' he said. 'But we shall have to fix something up, Sara. Would you consider changing your job? I know how devoted you are to St Saviour's, but...'

'They may be going to close my wards,' Sara said. 'I did think I might look for something in London.'

'I've leased a flat for six months,' Richard said. 'That gives us plenty of time to look for somewhere more permanent. We can manage somehow until you decide what to do.'

'Yes...'

Even Sara could hear the indecision in her voice, so it

wasn't surprising that Richard was giving her a hard look. She shook her head at him, letting her hair tumble on to his face.

'Don't pull a face,' she said. 'I think I'm going to make some coffee—and then I'll explain.'

She moved to leave the bed, but he caught her, pulling her down, trapping her beneath him so that she was forced to look up at him.

'Tell me now, Sara—don't keep me in ignorance. Why aren't you sure about moving in with me?'

'It's not that…' She couldn't keep her doubts out of her eyes. 'I want to, Richard, of course I do… It's just that I'm not sure…'

'Whether you love me enough to make a long-term commitment?'

'No, I'm sure of that,' she said and smiled. 'I'm not sure how you'll feel about my news…' She took a deep breath and told him what she suspected. For a moment, he didn't answer, just stared down at her. 'It's my fault,' she said. 'I should have told you I wasn't using anything. I just didn't think…'

Richard released her and sat up. He got out of bed and pulled on a dark blue robe, tying the lighter blue sash.

'You haven't done a test yet?'

'No, not yet. I didn't suspect anything until the other morning when I was checking my breasts for lumps. I noticed some changes. Nothing very much, just some gristle, I think. Then Angela told me I was looking tired. That made me realize how tired I actually was. I'd thought it was just that I hadn't been sleeping well, and I wasn't sure whether my period was late or not.'

'You've made an appointment to see your doctor?'

'Yes—but he can't fit me in for several days.'

'We'll get one before that. Jack will see you tomorrow.'

'I'm sure there's no need, Richard.'

'It could be a lot of things,' Richard said. 'I want to know for sure.' His eyes were dark with sudden fear for her. 'In view of your mother's history, I want that examination done tomorrow and you could also conduct your own pregnancy test.' He glanced at his watch. 'I should say this morning. I have to leave by six, Sara. I'm sorry, but the op I've promised for tomorrow is urgent. I can't put it off.'

'I don't want you to,' Sara said. She smiled, sitting up and holding out her hand to him. 'I have a good feeling about this, Richard. I'm ninety per cent sure I'm pregnant.'

Richard took her hand, sitting on the bed beside her. He turned her hand up to kiss the palm. 'And if you're right, what do you want to do?'

'I've decided I want to keep the baby,' Sara said. 'Unless you're very much against it?'

'Of course not! Good grief, why should I be?'

'Well, it is a little soon. I wouldn't have planned it this way…'

'No, I must admit I would have preferred some time to ourselves,' he said, and then grinned. 'This should please my sister. She's been on to me for ages to get myself a wife—now there will be a family in record time.'

'We're getting married?' Sara's heart beat wildly.

'Of course. What did you think I meant by a long-term commitment?' His brow creased. 'That's what you want—isn't it?'

'Yes.' Sara felt like jumping out of bed but she stayed

where she was and smiled up at him. 'Oh, yes, please. I would like that very much.'

'Good.' He lay down beside her again, then began to caress her breasts. She realized what he was doing and pushed his hands away. 'No, thank you, Doctor. I've already examined myself. Take my word for it, there are no definite lumps…just changes.' She kissed him on the lips, hard. 'Make love to me if you want, Richard—but you're not my doctor.'

Richard laughed, his hand sliding down her smooth thigh. 'All right, but you will ring me on my mobile as soon as you know? If I'm in surgery you can leave a message on the answering service.'

Sara nodded, then began to stroke his back. She nibbled at his shoulder, making him mutter, then laughed as he covered her with his body.

'Vixen,' he said. 'There's nothing wrong with your teeth, that's for sure.'

'There's nothing wrong with any part of me,' Sara assured him. 'Nothing that a little extra loving wouldn't put right…'

They married at the end of April, before Sara's gently rounded stomach became too obvious. Didn't want that on the wedding photographs! What would the children say when they were old enough to be inquisitive?

Angela thought it was wonderful, and so did Maureen, who sobbed all through the ceremony and kept looking accusingly at her own fiancé, who hadn't yet saved enough for the house he'd promised her.

Julia and Phyllis were both there, though Phyllis was looking pale and strained. She was still grieving for the loss of her baby, though her boyfriend was going ahead with the purchase of a cottage for them and they were going to live together. With any luck it wouldn't be long before Phyllis was pregnant again—and the chance of it going wrong a second time was remote.

Sara had given up her job at St Saviour's, leaving Staff Nurse Gillian Smith to take over in charge of the one remaining G ward the previous week. For the moment she wasn't looking for another job.

'I shan't stop you going back once the children are old enough to go to school,' Richard said. 'I know you want to specialize in Geriatrics, and if something positive comes along I'll back you all the way—but I would like you to be at home for a while.'

Sara hadn't argued. After working for most of her adult life so far, it would be good to have a little time off. She was looking forward to being just a wife and mum for a few years and, though she hadn't yet told Richard, she was beginning to suspect that she was carrying twins, which meant double trouble! Or double the fun, whichever way you looked at it. They were going to need that house with a garden Richard had set his heart on buying.

They had talked about wanting a girl and a boy, and with any luck they might get what they wanted in one fell swoop. She was going to tell Richard of her suspicions after their honeymoon, but not before. If he guessed that her pregnancy might not be as easy and straightforward as she'd led him to believe, he would never stop fussing over her—and they were going to Paris. Sara had always longed to go there but had never got round to it. She didn't intend to let anything stop her seeing it all!

'I don't much like lying on beaches and getting burnt to a cinder,' Sara had told him when they'd discussed where they would spend the six days which was all Richard could take off from his work, 'but I've always wanted to go to Paris.'

'Then that's what we'll do,' Richard had said, kissing her. 'I want to make you happy, darling.'

He had just bought her a beautiful engagement ring that afternoon, the first time she'd had a chance to join him in London.

'I was going to ask you to marry me the day Kurt turned up,' Richard had said ruefully. 'It was going to be a big surprise for after my interview. I thought we'd go shopping and look for a ring.'

'And then I went and spoiled it all,' Sara had said. 'What an idiot I was. Instead of almost three weeks of misery, I could have been wearing this.' She'd flashed the circle of white diamonds surrounding an emerald. 'It's beautiful, extravagant. I don't know what I've done to deserve something like this.'

'You'd better get used to it,' he'd said. 'There will be plenty more treats in store for you.'

'Oh, goody,' Sara had teased. 'I knew I was marrying you for some reason or other.' She'd paid for that remark later that evening, in a manner that Richard had devised, which seemed to give them both equal enjoyment.

Now, several weeks later, they were surrounded by their wedding guests as the bells rang out to announce their marriage to the world.

Sara had asked her stepfather to give her away, even going so far as to ask his new partner to the wedding. She was a pleasant woman as far as Sara could see, very quiet and rather plain. Not the seducer she had once imagined. The past was over, it was time to forget.

She was perfectly happy, there were no shadows hanging over her as she made her vows that sunny April morning.

'What are you smiling about?' Richard whispered as

they paused outside the church for the first of the photographs. 'Just what is going on in that head of yours?'

'Wouldn't you like to know?' she teased. 'As a matter of fact, I was just wondering what the bed will be like in our hotel in Paris... I hope it's nice and roomy.'

'Why?' Richard picked up the teasing note in her voice and gave her a wicked grin. 'Because I'll be sharing it with two of you?'

Sara laughed and shook her head at him.

Maybe three of us, she thought, but kept that thought inside. Just maybe...

MILLS & BOON®

Makes any time special™

Mills & Boon publish 29 new titles every month. Select from...

Modern Romance™   Tender Romance™

Sensual Romance™

Medical Romance™ Historical Romance™

MAT2

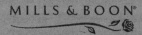

Medical Romance™

CLAIMED: ONE WIFE *by Meredith Webber*

Book two of The Australian Doctors duo

Neurosurgeon Grant Hudson knows that fraternisation between colleagues can break hearts, ruin careers and even lives. Yet for Dr Sally Cochrane, he is prepared to break his own rule. Sally, however, has her own reasons for keeping him out of her life...

A NURSE'S FORGIVENESS *by Jessica Matthews*

Book one of Nurses Who Dare trilogy

Marta Wyman is not going to let Dr Evan Gallagher pressurise her into meeting up with her grandfather. No matter how handsome, polite and charming Evan is he will have a long wait before she changes her mind—or gives in to her desires...

THE ITALIAN DOCTOR *by Jennifer Taylor*

Dalverston General Hospital

Resentment simmered between Luke Fabrizzi and Maggie Carr when her family tried to introduce them with marriage in mind. But a staged relationship in order to avert their families led to a truce—and another battle against their true feelings!

On sale 4th May 2001

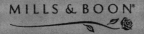

Medical Romance™

NURSE IN NEED by *Alison Roberts*

Emergency nurse Amy Brooks rushed into an
engagement when she realised she wanted a family of
her own—then she met Dr Tom Barlow. She had to
end the engagement and Tom was delighted—but was
his love for Amy the real reason?

THE GENTLE TOUCH by *Margaret O'Neill*

Jeremy is asked to persuade Veronica Lord into letting
him treat her. Just as he gains her trust, Jeremy
discovers that he was present when she had her
accident and could have helped her. Will she ever be
able to forgive him, let alone love him?

SAVING SUZANNAH by *Abigail Gordon*

Until Dr Lafe Hilliard found her, Suzannah Scott
believed she had nothing left. Lafe helped her to rebuild
her life and all he wanted in return was honesty. But if
Suzannah revealed her past, she risked not only losing
his professional respect, but his love…

On sale 4th May 2001

4 FREE

books and a surprise gift!

We would like to take this opportunity to thank you for reading this Mills & Boon® book by offering you the chance to take FOUR more specially selected titles from the Medical Romance™ series absolutely FREE! We're also making this offer to introduce you to the benefits of the Reader Service™—

- ★ FREE home delivery
- ★ FREE gifts and competitions
- ★ FREE monthly Newsletter
- ★ Exclusive Reader Service discounts
- ★ Books available before they're in the shops

Accepting these FREE books and gift places you under no obligation to buy, you may cancel at any time, even after receiving your free shipment. Simply complete your details below and return the entire page to the address below. *You don't even need a stamp!*

YES! Please send me 4 free Medical Romance books and a surprise gift. I understand that unless you hear from me, I will receive 6 superb new titles every month for just £2.49 each, postage and packing free. I am under no obligation to purchase any books and may cancel my subscription at any time. The free books and gift will be mine to keep in any case.

M1ZEA

Ms/Mrs/Miss/Mr ....Initials....................................
                                              BLOCK CAPITALS PLEASE
Surname ....
Address ....
....
....Postcode..................................

Send this whole page to:
UK: FREEPOST CN81, Croydon, CR9 3WZ
EIRE: PO Box 4546, Kilcock, County Kildare (stamp required)